Tough Enough

Ten Stories

Tough Enough

Ten Stories

Emily Hartzog

Tough Enough: Ten Stories

Emily Hartzog

"Firstborn" previously appeared in *Scarlet Leaf Review*, February/March 2021.

Cover image: *Return to the Root* by Cheryl Warrick © 2000. Carborundum, softground etching, aquatint, sugarlift, and monotype. Image/sheet: 31" x 22.5". Artist's proof; edition 4/4. Signed, titled, and dated recto. Published by Dolan/Maxwell; image courtesy of the artist and Dolan/Maxwell.

ISBN-13: 979-8746869753
ISBN-10: 8746869753

Copyright © 2021 by Emily Hartzog (Grapeseed Press).

All rights reserved. Except as permitted under the United States Copyright Act of 1976, no part of this publication may be reproduced or transmitted in any form or by any means, or stored in a database or retrieval system, without permission of the author. Printed in the United States of America.

Shall I dance them again, the nightlong dances?
Dance again with bare feet in the dew?
Shall I toss my head and skip through the open fields
as a fawn slipped free of the hunt and the hunters,
leaping their nets, outrunning their hounds?
She runs like a gale runs over the plain
near the river, each bound
and plunge like a gust of joy, taking her
dancing, deep through the forest
where no one can find her, and the dark
is free and its heart is the darkest green.

> Euripides, *The Bacchae*
> (trans. Robin Robertson)

CONTENTS

Spirits	1
Southern Discomfort	18
Firstborn	37
Lucky	60
Three Bullfights	83
Tough Enough	108
A Winter in Somerset	127
Rock with Wings	147
Nogales	173
Fear Not	194

SPIRITS

When I was very young, my father said, "Rosie, did you know your mother claims she saw an angel once? She says it was just before her father died."

My grandfather died before I was born, but I thought my mother would have told me if something that extraordinary had happened.

"Is it really true?" I asked.

"You should believe your mother. She swears she saw her."

I looked over at my mother who said, "I did see an angel, Rosie. Your father is the one who doesn't believe me. Now he's trying to get you to doubt me too."

She put her hands on my shoulders and said, "Someday, I'll tell you exactly what happened when my father died."

~~

That summer, we took a trip from North Carolina to South Carolina and stayed at a place called South of the Border just south of the state line. There was a giant statue of a man named Pedro wearing a big sombrero that you could see from the highway. When we drove through his legs into the parking lot, we saw painted animals that were bigger than our car. The photographs from the trip showed me dwarfed by at a gorilla in an orange T-shirt, a red dinosaur in a top hat, and a blue rabbit with antlers.

In the afternoon, I went with my mother to a shop called Day of the Dead. The shelves were full of skeletons dressed in all sorts of clothes and skulls with big smiles on their faces. My mother asked questions, and the Mexican woman behind the counter was excited to tell us about everything.

She told us that on the Day of the Dead, the living people cooked special food for all their dead relatives and sat in graveyards with flowers and candles all night to be close to them. I still remember her accent and her beautiful dark hair. I'd never seen anyone like her before. My mother bought a little skeleton dressed in a black suit that reminded her of her father, and the Mexican woman gave us candy skulls for free.

Later that day, my father took me to a colorful shop where he bought Mexican jumping beans for me from a pretty blonde lady. I kept them in my pocket for the rest of the trip. That night, we went to a place called a cantina with singing and dancing and drinks called Margaritas. My drink was called a *limonada*, and it had a green and red flag in it and a pink swizzle stick. I rolled them up in my napkin and took them with me when I left.

The next morning, I took my mother over to the jumping bean shop so I could show her a big camel with two humps I had seen the day before. I noticed my father in the back, standing close to the pretty lady, but he acted like he didn't know me. I wasn't sure if my mother saw him, but I remember looking away quickly because it seemed like a

SPIRITS

secret. I thought he was probably buying more beans to surprise me, but I never got them.

After our vacation, my mother fell down late one night. She often fell down when she was drinking and my father had to pick her up, but this time she broke her leg. She had to go to the hospital for surgery and needed to stay until she could walk with crutches.

My father and I ate a lot of sandwiches while she was away, and it seemed to take forever. We were so excited when she came home that we made her a cake. I drew a picture of our family with big smiles, and we taped it on the front door.

My handsome father was a traveling salesman, and my mother was a drinker. They did everything together, so I guess he must have been a drinker too. The very same week that my mother came home, my father left on a trip and never came back.

I've always wondered what happened since he never told me goodbye. I missed him. All I had left were the presents he'd brought to me from his trips over the years. I lined up them up on my dresser and kissed the trolls before I went to sleep.

~~

After my father left, my mother became fascinated with a world I couldn't see. She asked Jesus to help us get through our difficult time and talked to the angels who were looking over us. Since I hadn't started kindergarten yet, she read Bible stories to me in the mornings, and we ate Little Debbie cakes and watched Dark Shadows in the afternoons.

At night, she made Shirley Temples for me, and I decorated them myself with extra cherries. Late at night, after she'd been drinking, I sometimes heard her having conversations. Once when I crept out to see who she was talking to, no one else was there.

Some nights I heard her stumble, but I never had to pick her up. That was good since I wasn't sure I could. Many mornings, she was shut up in her room with a 'sick headache', and I knew better than to knock on the door until she felt better and came out to see me herself.

My mother's father had been able to make tables walk and hear spirits speak, and my mother, even as a young child, had been able to see ghosts, as well as angels. She said that her late aunt had appeared in a sparkly dress with silver tassels and danced around her room in a cloud of perfume. And her grandmother brought her cookies that were so delicious she could still taste them when she sat up.

"Did your grandmother dance too? I asked.

"No, her ghost was so faint I could see right through her, but I could smell the cookies."

"What kind of cookies were they?" I asked.

"They were warm chocolate chip cookies, so soft you could fold them in two," my mother said. "I've tried every recipe in the book, but I think only people in heaven can make them."

"Can you tell me about the time the angel visited your father before he died?" I asked.

SPIRITS

"I can," my mother said. She took a big swallow of her drink. I stirred the ginger ale with my pink swizzle stick and did the same.

She said that right before her father died, the angel floated down from the light above him. She had big lace wings and a ring of light around her head so bright you couldn't look directly at her face. The angel bent down and kissed his forehead, and he smiled at the moment that he died. She then saw his spirit float back up with the angel to the light.

I told her that I'd like to see an angel or a ghost.

"Well there's my friend Gloria now!" my mother said.

I looked at the chair she was pointing to, but I didn't see anything.

"Since she's dropped by, we should make her a drink," my mother said. "Go grab the other glass like mine and I'll pour some bourbon in it."

I brought it to the table, and my mother poured the bourbon. She said that I should watch the glass carefully because the bourbon would start to go down.

She told me that Gloria had a monkey who used to jump in her hair and mess it up. She said that once Gloria left the door open, and the monkey ran away from home and got lost.

I imagined a lost monkey knocking on doors trying to find Gloria. Suddenly, I was sure the liquid in the glass had gone down. "I see it! I see it! She *is* here!" I said.

My mother told me that her father always 'poured one out' for a visiting ghost, sending the alcohol spirit to the angels in their memory. She took Gloria's glass to the sink and closed her eyes, like she'd shown me to do when I was making a wish, then poured it all away. When she came back to the table, she said, "Here's to Gloria," and we both finished our drinks.

My mother told me that if you were saved by Jesus, when you died you could go back and forth between heaven and earth. And since you were invisible to most people, you could move around wherever you wanted. She said she wanted to make sure she was saved and would go to heaven. I thought it sounded fun to be invisible, so I wanted to be saved when I grew up too.

I knew a little bit about it because we watched Reverend Ernest Angelhart on Sundays and put our hands on the TV screen to touch his hand during the saving and healing part of his show. I wanted to be healed, because I sometimes had spells where my eyes rolled back in my head and I saw colors flashing. If I was walking, I had to sit down, even if it was on the ground.

My spells really scared me because I went to some other place when I had them and I never knew where I was when I woke up. My mother said they showed I was possessed by the spirit, but I wanted the spirit to leave me alone. When my spells happened, they also scared the people around me, especially my father. I've always wondered if that was why he left.

The next morning, my mother woke up just in time to see the Ernest Angelhart Show. I put my hand on the TV and tried as hard as I could to believe in his magic healing powers,

SPIRITS

but as soon as his prayer ended, I had another spell and had to lie down on the floor. I started to cry afterwards, but then the Reverend announced he was coming to Charlotte to heal all the people. Since it was close by, we decided we would go.

My mother was sure his powers worked much better when he actually touched you in person. She said that when we came home, we would be brand new. I would be healed, and she would know she was saved and could go to heaven. Then she would come back and visit me anytime, even after she died. I wondered why my mother wanted to go to heaven so early, but I closed my eyes and made a wish for both of those things to come true. I also made a secret wish that my father would return soon.

I was awake early on the day we were going to see Ernest Angelhart and burst into my mother's room and woke her up. I was surprised to find her sleeping on top of the covers in the same clothes as the night before. I asked her if she was okay, and she said yes, but I wasn't convinced enough to leave. She let me climb up and lie beside her for a while, and she told me about how the spirit would pass through the Reverend's healing hands and give us everything we needed.

She smelled of alcohol, cigarettes, and Shalimar perfume. Even now, any one of those three smells will remind me of her. I thought all the mysterious women we saw in the movies on TV must smell exactly the same way.

A few hours later, we were on our way to Charlotte. We wore our prettiest summer dresses, and I admired the pink nails that I'd helped my mother paste on the night before. We were in our old, red Toyota pickup truck. Mice ran out of the vents when we turned on the heat in winter, but it was July so they could rest easy. The air conditioner hadn't worked in years.

I liked to talk to the invisible mice when we were in the truck. I told them where we were going and how nice we looked. I had the Mexican jumping beans in my pocket for luck, so I took one out and held it in front of the vent for the mice to see. The beans hadn't jumped in a year, but every so often I still took them out to check for any signs of movement.

My mother was in a good mood. She poured bourbon from a flat silver flask into a cup, that she held between her legs. It was the one her father gave her when he died. We were both laughing a lot, and my mother said that two dressed-up girls in an old pickup truck must be mighty interesting to the men passing by.

Just about then, the truck sputtered and the motor turned off. My mother pulled over to the side of the highway and said, "Oh no, Rosie. We've run out of gas. I've never seen the dial fall to empty that fast."

"How will we get there with no gas?" I asked.

"We still have some minutes to spare before the Reverend starts," my mother said. "I got us into this mess, and I'll get us out of it. You stay in the truck and watch me work my magic."

She walked to the back of the truck, stuck out her hip and her thumb, and smiled and a nice man pulled over right away. They talked for a few minutes. She stood close to him, and I watched him rub her back to make her feel better. Then he drove away. Men always seemed to like my mother. She made them laugh a lot.

When she got back in the truck, she told me that he was going to bring us some gas, and it shouldn't take too long. The longer we waited, the hotter it got in the cab of the truck. Our hair started to get damp around the edges and there were wet spots on our clothes. My mother kept looking at her watch. I knew she was upset, because she forgot to pour the bourbon into the cup and drank it straight from the flask instead.

I was just telling the mice not to worry about how hot it was getting, when the nice man drove up with the gas can. My mother joined him as he poured the gas in the tank. I heard my mother saying, "Please, please!" I leaned out the window and saw him finally accept the money she was holding out. She yelled, "Thank you, Sweetie!", blew him a kiss, and we took off in a cloud of dust.

Since we weren't going to have time to eat lunch, we bought snacks at the gas station. I generally liked snacks much more than eating in restaurants and was excited to find my favorite Little Debbie cakes and a new kind of root beer I'd never seen. But once we started down the road, it was hard to eat or drink very much without making a big mess. My mother was passing everybody and driving so fast that I had to hold on to the seat, sometimes with both hands.

We pulled into the parking lot of the church just on time, but the lot was full and we had to park so far away that we were late. My mother said it was ninety degrees outside, and by the time we'd run to the door, we were both dripping wet. We used lots of paper towels in the bathroom to dry ourselves off, and my mother fixed the mascara smudges under her eyes and put on fresh lipstick.

When we came out of the bathroom, we found an usher who was eager to help. He apologized that the only seats left were in the back row and told us we could get better ones after the break. He had a crew cut and wore a spotless white shirt with a badge on it. He found us a place in the middle of a pew, so we had to squeeze past people to get there.

It was hard for me to see over the high-backed pews, so I mostly listened to the words. We were both excited, and my mother watched with great expectation. She occasionally leaned down to whisper about how pretty something was. We smiled at each other when Reverend Angelhart said that he had Healing Power straight from God and Resurrection Power that would grant Eternal Life. He also had special Blessed Cloths for sale, which healed you just by pinning them to the clothes you wore.

There were big electric fans in the aisles, but it was getting hotter and hotter. My mother fidgeted during the Sinner's Prayer where you promise God to give up nicotine and alcohol. The Reverend then told us that Jesus was coming soon and time was running out. To be a partner in Christ, he recommended a pledge of one hundred dollars or whatever you could afford. My mother whispered that she'd given most of her cash to the man who helped us with the gas, and she

SPIRITS

was beginning to think he deserved it more than the Reverend did.

"Do you have to pay to be healed?" I asked.

"It's looking like it," my mother said. "Do you want to leave?"

I didn't want to leave because I still wanted my spells to go away. If there were too many people who paid and got ahead in the Reverend's healing line, I figured at least we could buy a Blessed Cloth.

She said, "Okay, let's see what happens."

As soon as the break came, my mother said she needed to go back to the truck. I knew she still had some left in the silver flask and was headed there to drink it. During the break, I looked at the big stained-glass windows and moved my hands through the red and blue light. I also walked around looking for the Blessed Cloths and couldn't find them.

Since my mother hadn't yet returned, I went back in and found us better seats, in the front and near the aisle, so I would be able to see. I stood up in the pew facing backwards so I could wave to her when she came back. I figured she'd be easy to spot because of her bright pink dress. A few minutes later, a lady sitting in the row behind told me that I needed to sit down because they were about to begin.

~~

A choir came out in long white robes with big smiles. They stood in a big open space under a stained-glass window of a giant gold crown with a lamb underneath. They sang a song called *Jesus is Alive* and swayed and clapped to the music. I noticed that some people from the audience were already lined up to one side. I thought it must be the healing line since some of them were in wheelchairs, but I was too shy to join it by myself.

When Reverend Angelhart appeared, everyone got excited. They yelled 'Thank you Jesus!' and a few threw their heads back and made strange sounds I'd never heard before. I wondered if it was how you talked to the angels. The Reverend was dressed all in white and had lots of shiny hair. He asked if we were ready for the healing part of the service and everybody screamed, "Yes!"

He pointed to the white-haired lady in a wheelchair at the front of the line and said, "Mrs. Robbins, come and take your cure!" She rolled her chair over to him. He put his hand on her forehead and said, "Let the Holy Spirit flow through you. I command all the nerves and muscles to be recreated. Get up from that chair! Start walking! Walk again, right here, in front of everybody. The Lord has healed you through my hands." She got up and walked all the way from one side to the other, and the audience went crazy with joy.

Next in line was a teenage boy who had been deaf since he was born. The Reverend gave him a sharp whap on the forehead. He fell backwards and two ushers caught him. When the boy stood up again, Reverend Angelhart said, "Say COME IN JESUS! COME IN JESUS!" The boy yelled something, but it was hard to understand what he said. Again, the audience roared.

SPIRITS

Reverend Angelhart said that he had the Power of X-ray Vision. He was able to look into a person's body and see what needed curing. That was the gift the Lord gave him.

It was then that I saw my mother walk past me up the aisle. She was putting her feet down carefully like she had to think about every step. Her pink dress, which had looked so pretty in the morning, was now damp and wilted. Four of her paste-on nails were missing and she was wearing too much lipstick. The ushers tried to stop her, but she put her arms out and pushed past them.

She stood in front of the Reverend and said, "Please help me. I want to feel the holy spirit."

He said, "I'm sorry Ma'am. You need to wait your turn. There's a whole line of people waiting to get up here."

My mother started to cry, "I can't wait any longer. It will only take a minute. How could you refuse? I beg you to save me!"

Reverend Angelhart stared hard at my mother. I wondered if he was using his X-ray vision to see what she looked like inside.

He nodded to the ushers who moved in behind her. He put his hand on her forehead, gave her a sharp push, and said, "You are Saved. Praise the Lord!" She fell backwards, and the ushers caught her and stood her up. She turned her head to kiss one of them, but the usher moved his face away and she kissed his shirt instead.

Suddenly, she fell down again. Since the ushers weren't behind her anymore, she crumpled to the floor. One of them quickly helped her sit up, and the one she'd tried to kiss whispered something in the Reverend's ear.

Reverend Angelhart turned to the audience and said, "I've been told this woman has whiskey on her breath. She didn't fall down in the Spirit. She fell down because she was drunk." He turned to my mother and said, "Go away and come back when you repent!"

The ushers held her up by her arms and led her down the aisle. One of them was the same usher who had helped us before, so I stood up in the pew so he could see me. When they lowered my mother into the seat next to me, I saw the big lipstick smear on his white shirt.

My mother slumped over and went straight to sleep. Every now and then, she whispered my name, but I'm not sure she knew I was there. When it was over, I couldn't wake her up so everyone had to squeeze past us to get out. One man pointed to me and said to his wife, "That drunk woman has a child with her." I closed my eyes and tried as hard as I could to turn us into ghosts. That way, we could disappear and end up somewhere else. But it didn't work.

The church was almost empty by the time my mother started to wake up.

She said, "Rosie, what have I done? I messed up both our chances."

SPIRITS

I told her it wasn't true. I told her she had been saved, and I saw it with my own eyes. I held her hand while she quietly cried and watched them clean the front of the church. It looked so big and sad now that everyone was gone. The noise of the chairs scraping the floor made loud echoes behind us.

I felt angry when I saw the usher walk up the aisle past us. He told the workers to gather up all the leftover booklets and put them in the boxes at the back. His arms looked like skinny sticks poking out from his sleeves, and his pants were way too short. He noticed that we were still sitting in the pew, so he came to sit on the other side of my mother. The lipstick smear was still there on his white shirt.

He said, "We're going to have to be clearing out of here in about fifteen minutes."

My mother patted his arm and said, "I know, honey. You're such a sweet young man. Thanks for everything you've done."

I wanted to hit him, since he was the one who told the Reverend about the whiskey on her breath. She was thanking him after he had told on her in front of everybody.

He said, "I'm really sorry about what happened here today, but I know you can repent. I know you have the power inside you to change. We all do. I was a juvenile delinquent before I found Jesus. You could have a whole new life, just like me."

I didn't know the word *repent*, but I didn't like the sound of it. And I knew my mother didn't want a whole new life. She only wanted to be saved so that she could come back and visit me after she died. I stood up and told her I wanted to go home.

The usher asked, "How far is the drive home?"

My mother said, "Don't worry, I'll sleep it off in the truck before I leave."

On the way to the truck, we saw a little girl in shiny shoes tugging a furry dog on a leash. Her face was red from the heat and the dog was panting, but they looked happy. Her father was a few steps behind her. He stopped to stare at us as I helped my mother take the big step into the old pick-up, then shook his head and ran to catch up with his daughter and the dog.

It was very hot inside the truck. We opened all the windows, and my mother went straight to sleep. I watched her closely at first, worried she might wake up and need me for something. I felt sad about not being healed and tried not to cry as I sat there wondering what to do. After a few minutes, my attention turned to my stomach. It was growling because I'd missed lunch and now it was close to dinnertime.

The mice hadn't touched the wrapping left over from the Little Debbie cakes, and there was still some icing melted on the sides that I could see through the clear plastic packet. I used my finger to get everything that was left and tried not to smear the seat. Afterwards, I cleaned my hands and face with an old napkin I found on the floor of the truck.

SPIRITS

The silver flask was on the seat bedside my mother. I turned it upside down, and it was empty. I remembered I still had some of my root beer left, so I picked up the can and took a swallow. Even though it was hot, it still tasted good. I drank a little but decided to save most of it for my mother because I knew she was going to be thirsty when she woke up.

~~

My mother was never able to find the strength to repent, and she died earlier than she should have. When I turned eighteen, my spells went away on their own despite my not being healed by the Reverend when I was five. I was never able to see ghosts like my mother and grandfather could, so I never saw her again in person after she died.

I don't drink anymore, but I still keep some bourbon in the silver flask. Every time I feel my mother close by, I make her a drink in the glass she always liked. Then I pour it down the sink and send her spirit to the angels when I can no longer smell her perfume.

SOUTHERN DISCOMFORT

Her mother opened the door and turned on the light. "It's time for you to get up and get ready for book club. You promised last night you'd come down and meet everybody."

Ellen put a hand up to shield her eyes. "I was drinking when I promised. You waited to catch me at a weak moment. I'm still hungover. I need more sleep. I can't even think about standing up and taking a shower yet."

"I'm asking you to do one thing for me. You might think about all I've done for you over the years. We're reading *Isle of Palms* and it's such a nice book. My friends would be overjoyed to see you, Miss Princess, if you could only grace us with your presence." Her South Carolina drawl deepened with her sarcasm.

Ellen made her mind blank in an effort not to react and looked past her mother, out the back window of her bedroom. She'd opened it earlier thinking fresh air might do the trick. The pungent scent of fall had filled the room but hadn't done much for her headache. Max, her spotted spaniel, was nosing around in the leaves and digging in the dirt.

"I hate that syrupy stuff. There's no way my stomach could take an hour of y'all dredging up memories of your pampered Southern childhoods."

"Well, I've got something to tell you young lady. You're Southern before you're American in this house."

Ellen looked around the room with its lace coverlets, mahogany bookshelves, and rose patterned wallpaper. She put a feather pillow over her head and screamed underneath it.

"May I remind you that your great-great-grandfather fired the first shot of the Civil War and had a plantation with 200 slaves? He had a military diploma from the Sovereign State of South Carolina." Ellen's mother had blonde hair combed into a tight helmet and a Junior League scarf tied around her neck. Her face always looked set for battle.

Ellen moaned into her feather pillow, "We should be ashamed of that history, not proud of it."

"How did I end up with a Yankee daughter? It boggles my mind. You must have Yankee friends at boarding school who've filled your head with this nonsense."

Ellen took the pillow off her head and began to sing, *"In the beauty of the lilies Christ was born across the sea. With a glory in His bosom that transfigures you and me."*

"You know I hate that abomination of a Yankee song, and I never want to hear it again in my house. Now stop that infernal singing immediately, get in the shower, and get downstairs."

"As he died to make men holy, let us die to make men FREE! His truth is marching on."

Her mother stormed out the door before she could launch into the Glory Hallelujahs.

Ellen had no intention of going downstairs, but she did want to take a shower. She rearranged the pillows and smoothed down the sheets, so the bed would look inviting when she came back. She tiptoed down the hall in her bathrobe and stopped by the window above the front porch so she could see which of her mother's friends were there. The women were all dressed similarly in light silk blouses, brightly colored jackets, and matching shoes; outfits bought at the new Talbots shop in town.

Max wagged his tail as each guest came onto the porch, but they didn't notice him. They were too engrossed in their polite greetings, with fixed mannequin-like smiles plastered on their faces.

The shower helped a little, and she was just settling down again in bed when she heard her mother call from downstairs. "Darling, we're starting to eat now so you should come down and join us."

Ellen hesitated, then decided it was less trouble to yield to the unavoidable. She yelled down, "Okay Mother."

She ran a brush through her wet hair which hung in strings around her face and pulled an oversized sweater over her flimsy peach nightgown and shoved her feet into some flipflops. On the way downstairs, she noticed some remnants of black polish on her toenails that looked like dirt in the corners.

The six women with their scarves, pins, and carefully styled hair remarked on how wonderful Ellen looked. Their pearls glistened, and bracelets tinkled on their slender wrists. They oozed Southern charm.

Mrs. Gilliam asked, "How are things going at St. Catherine's? My niece loved it there."

"I'm enjoying it—particularly since North Carolina is more progressive. It's a breath of fresh air." Ellen said. This seemed to quieten them down. She waited for a response.

Her mother said, "North Carolina has always been too progressive. It's hardly a Southern state compared to South Carolina and Virginia."

Ellen asked Mrs. Gilliam, "How do you like this month's book? My mother says it's great and *so* nostalgic."

She laughed, "I love the wonderful books we pick out about the South, but it's hard to find the time to finish them. Didn't your mother tell you? This is mostly a drinking club—we only call it a book club for cover."

During dinner, the ladies polished off five bottles of wine as if they were nothing more than a pitcher of sweet tea. As soon as Ellen was sure they were done with quizzing her and were deep into local gossip, she decided she'd made enough of an appearance and could safely leave. She said she had a headache and went back upstairs to bed. Max came with her and looked relieved when she closed the door behind them. He jumped on the bed and settled in for the night.

Before Ellen went to sleep, she repeated her mantra for trying to stay sane in this house: *Friends are the family you choose for yourself.* She would be back to her friends at school soon.

A group of girls in her class were making plans to go to the State House for the Equal Rights Amendment debate on the Senate floor, and she couldn't wait to be there to support it. They had practiced their cheers and ordered T-shirts, which were going to arrive when she got back.

~~

The next morning the sun filled the kitchen as Ellen fried bacon and stirred cheese grits on the stove. She'd cut the toast thick, and the eggs were mixed with cream in a bowl waiting to be scrambled, the way her mother liked them.

She knew she was doing this out of guilt for having been unpleasant to her mother the day before. Ellen's father had left with another woman some years ago, and her brother Edward lived with his girlfriend in a trailer somewhere in Florida and never called. At this point, Ellen was the only real family her mother had.

After a while, her mother appeared, looking sleepy, in a floor length robe and said, "You seem to be feeling quite a bit better this morning. Did you start with our leftover champagne?"

"I thought I'd make breakfast for us," Ellen said, "I'm sorry about yesterday."

"Don't worry. I'm used to it. My main job as a mother was to *civilize* my children, and I've obviously failed." It was said without a shred of humor. Her mother looked as hungover as Ellen had been the day before. They all drank too much in this family.

Her mother shivered and pulled her plush robe tighter, "Do you think you could find some time today to go with me to put flowers on Mother's grave? The fact that today's her birthday may have slipped your mind."

"Sure, Mom. And I did remember today was her birthday." Lying came easily to Ellen; a longtime habit when talking to her mother.

That afternoon the clouds drifted in, and the air got cooler. On the way to the graveyard, they stopped by the local florist and bought yellow roses. When they got back in the car, her mother reminded Ellen that her grandmother's money had made boarding school possible. Ellen said she would always be grateful, and she was being honest for a change.

Ellen liked going to the graveyard. The headstones sat peacefully in the grass, and the trees and gently rolling hills often appeared in her dreams. Her family had lived a long time in the area, so the old gravestones were interesting with their dates and names. When they arrived, the soft light made the hills, covered with pedestals, angels, and windowless mausoleums, seem even more dramatic.

The spell was broken when they got to the family plot.

"What are all these new things doing here?" Ellen asked. Small Confederate flags stood in cylindrical cups attached to the molded stone crosses at the feet of the family's oldest graves.

"Some vandals stole every beautiful, old Confederate cross in this graveyard, but the state replaced them. The crosses are new and not nearly as nice, but at least they added the flags."

"I hate the flags! They're offensive to so many people. Can't we take them away?"

"Are you going to start singing that damn Yankee song again? No! We can't just take them away. I want them here, and your great-great grandfather and his father and brothers would want them here, too."

Ellen's mother carefully cleaned her mother's bronze plaque with a wet cloth and laid the roses across it. They would probably be dead by the morning, but she didn't seem to care.

On the way back to the car, Ellen found herself stepping in time to the continuous loop of *Glory, Glory Hallelujah* running through her head. She was hatching a plan to steal all the Confederate flags in the graveyard that evening, put them in a garbage bag full of rocks, and sink them in the lake. Back at home, she started gathering the things she needed to execute her plan.

At dusk, she grabbed the spare set of car keys and brought Max along so she could use the excuse of walking her dog at the graveyard. The task turned out to be easy because no one else was around, and there were only thirty little flags in the whole graveyard.

After putting the last flag in the garbage bag, she and Max drove to the lake, which was also completely deserted. Everyone in the lakeside community must have been inside eating dinner. Ellen hoped they were looking at their food and not out the windows.

She waded up to her waist in the freezing water and threw the garbage bag out as far as she could. Max jumped in to retrieve the bag, but gave up when it sank, and came quickly back to shore. Ellen scratched Max's ears and congratulated herself on what a good deed they'd done. They headed home getting mud and water all over her mother's car.

When Ellen got home, her mother was watching the evening news with a gin and tonic in her hand.

Ellen said, "Mom, I took Max to the lake. He chased a duck into the water and got tangled up in some weeds, so I had to go and save him. I need to clean off the mud he got on the car." She grabbed some towels and dishwashing liquid.

Her mother said, "Max must be getting old. He's usually such a good swimmer. How *adult* of you to clean up. Maybe there's some hope of civilizing you after all."

In the two days remaining before she went back to school, Ellen listened to the local radio station as much as she could and read the local newspaper from cover to cover. She found no mention of the missing flags—good that she had gotten away with it, but bad that apparently no one had noticed.

~~

She had only been back at school a week when she received an emergency message to call her mother. On her way to the phone, she resolved to deny stealing the flags, no matter what evidence her mother might give.

Her mother sounded terrible on the other end. She said, "Ellen, you've got to get a bus ticket and come home right away. Your brother's in the Intensive Care Unit in Jacksonville and they need us there. I can't go down without you."

Ellen said, "Don't worry, I'll get the first bus tomorrow morning, but since it has so many stops, I probably won't get there until late. I'll call you from the bus station and let you know what time. How far is it to Jacksonville?" She cursed under her breath while her mother found a map. The ERA debate in Raleigh was to take place in two days. There was no way she could make it back there in time.

Her mother said, "It should be about six hours. You can rest, and then we'll start first thing day after tomorrow. I'm so upset I don't think I could make the trip on my own."

The next morning, Ellen sat glumly on the bus and realized that, although she felt upset about the whole situation, she was far from being the saddest person aboard. Many of the passengers wore looks of resignation that seemed to involve more than just the dreary journey. They carried paper bags of food, flattened pillows, and plastic bags stuffed with clothes. The only happy person was a little girl in pajamas. She smiled and waved at everyone after her mother fell asleep when the bus started up.

Ellen had packed almost nothing for the trip. She had convinced herself that if she were deliberately unprepared, maybe the trip wouldn't last too long. She hadn't even brought her schoolbooks, despite the fact she had exams coming up in two weeks. She hoped this might give her a good excuse to return to school after only a couple of days away.

Ellen had thought she was safe from her family in boarding school, but her twenty-seven-year-old brother had upended her life again. Weren't all the previous years of turmoil enough? She was jealous of her father who'd made the wise choice to abandon this emotional roller coaster five years ago. He and his new wife certainly would not be coming to Florida. She doubted they would even attend her brother's funeral if he died.

She never heard from her brother Edward. If someone called about him, it was always bad news—like this, often involving a hospital or a jail. Her mother somehow put up with all his disasters, shedding agonized tears but uttering no word of complaint. She handled Edward with kid gloves and never scolded him about his wayward behavior. And yet, when she had overheard Ellen say *shit* to one of her friends at school, she called Ellen a trash mouth and refused to speak to her for two weeks.

One of Ellen's few clear memories of her early childhood was of what her mother told her, sitting at the old kitchen table, after she had taken Edward to the psychiatrist for his violent temper tantrums. Her mother, choking with emotion, told Ellen that what she learned from the doctor was that Edward would have done better if he'd been an only child. She said she agreed with the psychiatrist, but how could she have known not to have another child? Ellen hadn't ever thought that she could be the source of Edward's problems, but she wondered if it was true for quite a few years.

Thinking back on that day, Ellen felt deeply angry. Many hours of her childhood were spent shut up in her room with her fingers in her ears trying to drown out the bitter arguments going on outside her door. Edward's favorite refrain was, "I didn't ask to be born!" She sure as *shit* didn't ask to be born, either.

~~

Ellen's mother picked her up at the bus station and apparently had plenty to drink before she got there. At home, they ate Stouffer's lasagna for dinner, and her mother went early to bed. Ellen sat in the kitchen with Max and sipped the last of her can of beer. It was clear that her mother wasn't dealing well with the situation and needed Ellen for support. Ellen tried to put aside her disappointment over missing the ERA debate. At least she had the T-shirt.

She decided to investigate her brother's room, without a clear idea what she was looking for. Max followed her into the room, stepped cautiously on the floor, and sniffed nervously in the corners. Edward had left a number of guns and knives in his dresser drawers, but she figured he had also brought plenty of weapons with him to Florida.

Her mother had hung a photograph of their grandfather on the wall across from the bed. She'd named Edward after her father who died of alcoholism when she was only six years old. That name may not have been such a good idea, but her mother liked it. She often said they had the same mischievous twinkle in their eyes.

Ellen found a folded Confederate flag stuffed in a bottom drawer and a few old flyers for Civil War reenactments underneath it. Edward was exactly the sort of chest-pounding loser the old sick South produced. He was armed to the teeth, alcoholic, and on welfare. That was 'mischievous', all right.

The next morning, her mother said she was too distraught to drive. She'd gotten a call from the hospital that Edward was doing worse. Ellen was relieved to be the one driving. She knew that she'd make better time than her mother and could use having to concentrate as an excuse not to talk. She tailed the fastest trucks on the interstate and cut more than half an hour off the drive.

The hospital in Jacksonville was a stark white building five stories high that looked like bad news. The interior was a maze of depressing hallways and chipped green walls. The staff pointed them down the hallway to the ICU.

At the ICU central station, one of the nurses took them to Edward's room and said she would call the doctor and find out when he could come by to talk to them. When her mother asked if Edward was doing better, the nurse just repeated that the doctor would be in soon. When she reminded them that the ICU allowed only two visitors at a time, Ellen remembered that Edward had recently lived with a girlfriend. She was obviously out of the picture since she was nowhere to be found.

It was strange to see Edward in the ICU, not only since he was hooked up to all those tubes, but also because he was so much younger than the other patients there. His eyes were closed, and he didn't respond when Ellen's mother grasped his hand. A ventilator was breathing for him, a tube coming from his nose had dark black clumps inside, and bags of fluid hung with lines leading to white bandages on his arm and chest. His gowned stomach was swollen like a beach ball and felt taut when Ellen touched it.

After a while, the nurse came to suction the ventilator tube in Edward's mouth. This led to a frantic fit of zombie-like coughing that was difficult to watch. The nurse told them the doctor would return for ICU rounds after his office hours had finished. Ellen went downstairs to get some food for them, but she guessed her mother would be too upset to eat.

When the doctor finally arrived, he was one of those somber types with grey hair, a pressed white coat, and a face deeply lined with wrinkles. He said that Edward had severe cirrhosis of the liver from alcoholism and was hospitalized because he vomited up a lot of blood. Ellen watched her mother wince when the doctor said *vomit*. It was one of the forbidden words in her house.

Ellen asked, "Is that why his stomach is so big?"

The doctor said, "Well, it's related. When the liver clogs up, the abdomen fills with fluid called ascites. The ascites is Edward's biggest problem now, because it's become infected and has in turn infected his whole body."

There was an uncomfortable silence. Ellen's mother was clearly stunned and incapable of asking questions. Ellen decided to take over. She asked, "Has the infection gotten better at all?"

"Not really. Even though he's young, we're not sure he's going to make it."

"Is there anything else you can do to help him make it?" she asked.

"We're trying one last antibiotic right now. If we could get the infection under control, and he abstained from alcohol from now on, he might be a candidate for a liver transplant. But right now, he's in bad shape and could die at any time. I just want to make sure you're prepared." The doctor extended his hand to them then moved on to take care of another ICU patient.

Ellen wondered what she could do to be more prepared. And most of all, how could she possibly prepare her mother? She found a hotel for them to stay within walking distance of the hospital, but it didn't look safe enough to walk anywhere around there.

Her mother was a wreck. Her make-up had dissolved with all the tears in smudges around the top of her white silk blouse, and the red veins in her cheeks were showing through. Her mascara was gone, and the bright red lipstick she usually wore had disappeared, leaving her lips deathly pale.

Ellen went to get the things from the car and poured her mother a Scotch over a glassful of ice. She grabbed a beer for herself and was glad there were five more because she knew she was going to need them. She ordered take-out from an Outback Steakhouse that she'd seen down the road and brought it back to the room. She ate some of the grilled chicken Caesar, but her mother would take nothing.

"Mom, you've got to try to eat something."

"I can't. I can't do anything but sit here and think about how awful this is. They say the worst tragedy that can happen to you is losing a child."

"Maybe you should take a bath and try to lie down. It might make you feel better."

"I told you, *nothing* is going to make me feel better. How could you talk about feeling better at a time like this?"

Ellen wanted to let loose at her mother for everything but managed to keep her feelings in check. She took a bath instead, and it calmed her down. She drank another beer and noticed it was starting to get dark outside.

She said, "Edward's in such bad shape that it doesn't look to me like he could get better. I doubt he could stop drinking to qualify for a liver transplant."

Her mother said, "You've never believed in your brother."

Ellen said, "You know he tried to poison me with insecticide in a ginger-ale bottle when I was five. Lots of times when you and Daddy went out for the night, he would lock me in closets and threaten me with guns and knives. I always knew he was trouble, but you just looked the other way."

"I know you never loved your brother. Now it sounds like you want him to die," her mother said.

"Maybe his life is so miserable that he wants to die. He's been running away and ending up in ditches since he was fourteen. Your whole life has been spent worrying about him."

"That's my concern, not yours, young lady. You may want him to die, but I want him to live. If he dies, I'll never get over it."

"The doctor said we have to prepare ourselves for the possibility of him dying. I'm just trying to help you."

"Well, you're not," her mother said and broke down in tears.

Ellen poured her another drink and opened another beer. After that, she fell asleep. When she woke up in the morning, her mother was sitting in exactly the same place by the window.

Ellen felt strangely disappointed there hadn't been an emergency call during the night. She just wanted the whole thing to be over with. Edward looked terrible, and he wasn't going to quit drinking. If he wasn't going to die now, it would probably happen in the near future; from disease or violence or whatever. She didn't want to go through this sort of thing again.

The first thing her mother said when she realized Ellen was awake was, "I've failed as a mother."

Ellen said, "No, Edward failed as a son."

"I don't mean him. I mean you. You're cruel and heartless."

Ellen didn't defend herself because she thought maybe her mother was right. They dressed and drove to the hospital in silence. They arrived at the ICU to meet the doctor on his morning rounds. The doctor nodded at them from the central station, indicating he would be along shortly.

Edward looked the same to Ellen. Her mother grasped his unresponsive hand and did not let go. It wasn't long before the doctor arrived. He seemed to be in a better mood.

He said, "I'm happy to say Edward is responding to the new antibiotic and had no fevers overnight. His blood work has improved, so it's possible he may pull through. We should be able to get him off the ventilator before too long if everything keeps going in the right direction. But he's still not out of the woods as far as the cirrhosis is concerned."

Her mother seemed reassured by the good-sounding news. She thanked the doctor repeatedly and shook his hand. Ellen wasn't sure how she felt. She had many questions about what to expect for her brother's recovery, but she didn't dare ask them in front of her mother. She thanked the doctor for all he had done.

As soon as he left, Ellen's mother turned to her and said with a sneer, "I guess you're disappointed that Edward is better now."

When Ellen didn't respond, her mother said, "I've thought about it all night and have decided that I can handle this situation better on my own and will be perfectly capable of driving home. There must be a bus that goes from Jacksonville to Raleigh. I can take you to the bus station whenever you find one."

Ellen said, "Mom, I would be happy to stay and help."

Her mother said, "You haven't helped. You're the only family I had left to help me through this crisis, but I would have been better off with no one at all. You wanted your brother dead because he was disrupting your petty little life. You should think hard about what the word *family* means. You'll have plenty of time on the bus."

The nighttime bus trip was going to take at least eleven hours, and Ellen did plan to do some thinking as well as trying to get some sleep. Being a disappointment to her mother was certainly nothing new. She'd spent her whole life wondering why, no matter how hard she tried, she never managed to do anything right.

Her mother didn't get out of the car or kiss her goodbye at the station, so Ellen didn't turn around to wave goodbye. She bought a big bag of Fritos and settled in the seat behind the driver. The bus was almost empty, and she had the seat to herself. She'd never been happier to be on the move—the further away, the better.

The more Ellen thought about the word *family*, the sadder she got. Her mind wandered to *Anna Karenina*, a book she had just finished at school. Tolstoy said that *each unhappy family is unhappy in its own way*. It occurred to her that her family was unhappy in *every* way, from her father to her mother to her brother, and she couldn't do anything about it.

A week after she got back to school, they told Ellen her mother was on the phone for her. When she picked up, her mother said Edward had died at home soon after leaving the hospital. She asked if Ellen was happy with the news.

FIRSTBORN

Beth left her home and her parents at seventeen and moved to the country. It was her first spring in the canyon, and she thought there had never been such a beautiful day. The new green leaves on the cottonwoods by the creek looked fluorescent in the sun, and the red canyon walls against the blue sky looked like a postcard. Through the window of her trailer, she saw several trees with flowers near the main house. Maybe it was an old orchard, but she couldn't be sure. She didn't know one tree from another, much less what a fruit tree looked like.

She was in love and had no doubt she'd made the right decision, in spite of what her parents said. Leaving them to live with Caleb and his family on the ranch had been like wiping the slate clean and starting over. Why she'd needed to start over at seventeen was another matter.

She dreaded telling her parents she was pregnant, but Caleb was excited about it. He'd started pestering her to move as soon as she broke the news. Her infatuation with Caleb began when she started high school, but he was a year ahead of her and seemed unattainable. She'd heard that Caleb brought sheep to the Sale Barn on Saturdays, so she started going there for lunch with her friend Gail. After many bowls of green chili stew, she finally caught his eye. Now that her dream had come true, she wanted to do all she could to make him happy.

Caleb's parents, Isaac and Rebecca Tucker, had been kind to her since she'd arrived. Caleb was their oldest child at eighteen, and they had seven other children, so there hadn't been many long conversations. In fact, there'd been no mention of the pregnancy yet. Food was not plentiful at their ranch, and she worried about the Tuckers having to feed yet another arrival.

Caleb and Beth lived in a rusted, white one-bedroom trailer across the way from the house. The Tucker house had been built a hundred years ago and didn't look big enough to sleep seven children and two adults, but somehow, they made it work. The main room had two long tables that took up most of the space. When all the family came in for dinner at the end of the day, everyone grabbed a folding chair from the stack in the corner.

The Tucker family labored from sunup to sundown on the ranch, and most of the work was centered around the crops and the animals. There were water gates which controlled the roaring flow in the main ditch which then led to the cross ditches. A complicated system of lesser ditches followed, finally ending in hundreds of small rivulets providing water for the acres of grass and alfalfa. Much time was spent getting the water to flow the right way. Sometimes Caleb was out there with a shovel all day.

The younger children took care of the animals. There were chickens, goats, and sheep to feed, horses to grain, and cattle to hay. Two spotted pigs ran wild, and large birds called guinea hens flew from tree to tree. There were assorted cats and dogs; some with names and some just referred to by their color.

She tried to do her part. When she'd struggled to milk the cow, five kittens had gathered round. One of them climbed in the pail and got sprayed by the one small trickle she finally coaxed from the udder. The kitten licked its fur and waited for more, but Beth was unable to produce it with her small hands. Caleb said not to worry because milking was hard and there were plenty of easier chores. She was disappointed because she'd always wanted to milk a cow.

Beth had a lot to learn. She found that even the simplest chore like gathering the eggs could be difficult. One morning a hen had pecked her hand and drew blood when she tried to get the eggs from her nest. Beth could see from the steely look in the hen's eyes that there was no moving her, so she went back to the trailer with only a few eggs to show for her labor. Caleb laughed, went back, picked up the squawking hen and found twenty eggs underneath her. He told Beth all about broody hens when they got back.

Her favorite dog was a Rottweiler-mix named Gus. He let the five kittens climb all over him and go to sleep on his back and across his shoulders. She'd taken a picture with her phone and sent it to her friend Gail in town.

Everyone she knew lived in Cortez, a town on the border of the Navajo Reservation, where Beth grew up. Beth and Caleb both went to Cortez High School, which was thirty miles from the Tucker ranch in McElmo Canyon. Cortez was a small town with two hunting stores across the street from each other and a few bars and pawn shops on the periphery. McElmo Canyon was right underneath the Ute Mountain and one of the oldest settled areas in the region.

Beth's father was an archeologist, originally from Denver, who worked exploring the Native American ruins in McElmo Canyon, and her mother taught American history at the high school. Beth had grown up with discussions of ranchers, public lands, and Native Americans at the dinner table.

Her family hiked on the weekends, but Beth was disappointed they didn't camp. They had a sheepdog, Otis, who Beth loved when she was a child, but they weren't able to housebreak him, so they gave him away. She never felt her parents were totally comfortable with animals or with the outdoors.

When Beth first started dating Caleb, her mother made an appointment so she could discuss birth control with a doctor. Her mother even picked up the birth control pills from the pharmacy every month and left them in Beth's room.

Beth punched them out and flushed them down the toilet since Caleb didn't want her to use them. She was happy to go along. She figured that way she would have him forever.

Her parents shed lots of tears when she told them she was leaving. They were standing in the kitchen making breakfast when Beth finally had the courage to tell them she was moving. It took both of them by surprise.

Her mother, who was usually so calm and collected, said, "You're crazy! You can't possibly want to do that."

Beth said, "I'm not crazy. I want to live with Caleb."

Her father said, "Moving to the Tuckers is a terrible idea. They're religious fanatics who barely eke out a living. If they didn't have land, they'd have nothing."

Her mother wept and her father tried to comfort her. Beth was surprised to see him crying too. He took off his glasses to wipe his eyes.

Eventually, her sad parents finally accepted the inevitable. They even volunteered to give her one of their old cars so she could come back and visit. She felt guilty driving away and wished she had a sibling, so they'd have somebody else to worry about when she was gone.

After the move, Beth decided to limit her time with her best friend Gail to only their classes, because she didn't want anyone to know she was pregnant. Gail asked lots of questions about Caleb and the Tuckers because of their reputation for being backwards and religious, but Beth was so stingy with information that she finally gave up. Gail even asked if she could come and visit the ranch, but Beth said she needed to get to know the Tuckers better first.

Gail and Beth had been best friends since grammar school. They both loved animals and dreamed of having farms when they grew up. Gail was excited to come with Beth to the Sale Barn on Saturdays because she loved to walk around the dirt stalls to look at the sheep and the cattle. They carefully chose the clothes they were going to wear ahead of time. They pulled on Wrangler jeans, wore Carhart shirts, and tried to act like they belonged.

It felt awful to have such a big secret, but Beth figured it was going to be easier for everybody if she kept the pregnancy to herself. That way, when her parents asked questions, Gail could be truthful when she said she didn't know the answers.

Beth wondered when her parents were finally going to realize that she was living the life of their dreams. Why couldn't they see that the Tuckers *were* American history? They had waist-high caves on their ranch where their ancestors hid from the Indians, eating grass and hunting prairie dogs for weeks at a time. And the Native American ruins that her father studied stretched out right behind their fences.

The Tuckers belonged to a religious sect called the Church of the Firstborn and didn't believe in doctors or the modern world. All eight children had been delivered by their father Isaac at home. Actually, there'd been nine children. The last baby got stuck, and after Isaac pulled him out, he was only able to move his head. They tried hard to keep him alive at home, but he died after only one month. Rebecca spoke often about the loss.

Beth knew about the home delivery and baby's death before she'd ever talked to Caleb. After the baby died, the news traveled fast from the Sale Barn. People felt it was a tragedy that didn't have to happen, so it was common knowledge in no time.

Beth and Caleb hadn't discussed where she was going to have the baby yet.

One morning, Beth was absentmindedly looking out the trailer window at Gus with the kittens on his back when she noticed one was missing. She went outside and looked for it everywhere, but it was nowhere to be found. When she mentioned it to Caleb that afternoon, he said that a coyote or a mountain lion had probably gotten it. Beth found that hard to believe since she thought the dog would have raised a ruckus if a mountain lion or coyote were inside the fence.

Over the course of a week, three more kittens went missing and she was distraught. She searched for them all over the farm and mentioned it to Caleb, but he didn't seem too interested. Gus wasn't too bothered either. The one remaining kitten seemed not to notice and continued to sleep on his back or in the crook of his leg.

The next week, Caleb came in laughing and said, "I figured out what was going on with them kittens you've been worrying about. Gus has been eating them himself. I saw him chomp down the last one this morning on the way to the barn."

Caleb was a big, handsome young man with his mother's brown eyes and olive skin. That afternoon was the first time she'd seen his father in him; a hard, defiant man determined to be as tough as any Tucker who came before.

At the beginning of May, there was much discussion during the family dinner about going to 'sheep camp'. From what Beth could gather, they needed to move the sheep up to the mountains where it was cooler in the summer and there would be more grass for grazing. Some of the Tucker family was going to herd the sheep up there on horseback, a trip of thirty miles that took several days. And some would go in the truck with the supplies and set up camp in the high meadows.

Beth was too nervous to ride a horse that far and had never herded anything in her life. She also figured it wouldn't be safe with the pregnancy. She pretended to be just as excited as the rest of them and secretly wondered about where you went to the bathroom and where everyone would sleep.

The land in the Rockies where the Tuckers had their summer grazing rights had been the same for over fifty years. These were different from their ditch rights, which set down in writing how much water the ranch was allowed. Since water was sometimes scarce, it was a constant topic of conversation. The Tucker ditch rights took precedence over almost everyone else in the canyon since the family had lived in the same place for so long.

Every rancher was responsible for taking care of the fences on his summer grazing land, so his livestock stayed where they should. He was also responsible for maintaining his portion of the ditch, so the water flowed freely. Those who didn't were bad-mouthed and threatened with guns.

Beth had figured out this much so far, but she often got confused during the heated conversations about who did what to whom.

She rode in the truck with Rebecca and three of the boys to the sheep camp. They towed a horse trailer full of supplies down endless dirt roads, each with a steeper bend than the one before, and finally arrived at a meadow near the top. It was covered in blue Columbine flower and red Indian Paintbrush, and the white aspens formed a wood of shimmering leaves on the far side. The simple cabin and fire pit were dwarfed by the towering Rockies behind them streaked with spring snow.

The first order of business was to check the fence before the animals got there. The bottom two strands of barbed wire needed to be tight because the sheep were notorious for escaping and getting into trouble. Isaac always said that sheep were born looking for a place to die.

Beth set off with confidence to check the fence, following it for a long distance until she found a strand of broken bottom wire. But how could she describe where it was located when she didn't even know which direction she was facing or what field she was in? She wandered back to help Rebecca unpack the truck. She didn't mention the broken fence because she figured someone else would find it.

She asked Rebecca, "Where's the bathroom? Inside the cabin?"

"Come with me," Rebecca said. They walked over to a tree that had a deep hole covered by a toilet seat behind it. "There are two of these. The other is over there," she said and pointed to another small tree. "You can always find them because you'll hear the flies in the daytime, and you can smell your way to them at night," she laughed.

"And does everyone sleep in the cabin?" Beth asked. Her bathroom and bedroom in the trailer had changed in her mind from seeming sad to seeming luxurious.

"Oh no. No one does. There are way too many mice. They'd run over you all night long, not to mention the snakes. We sleep outside in sleeping bags this time of year, right near the fire, so we don't get stomped on by a bear."

In the late afternoon, the rest of the Tuckers rode in with the sheep. Ellie, the youngest at six, was excited because she had ridden in front of Caleb on his horse all the way for three whole days. When she gave Beth a kiss, Beth noticed that the scar on Ellie's forehead, from falling off a horse last year, was red from the sun. Beth winced remembering the story of how Isaac made Ellie lie down on the kitchen table and stitched her up with a needle threaded with dental floss. Rebecca said Ellie was so brave she didn't even cry.

Isaac told Rebecca that herding the sheep along the roads went pretty much as usual, with one of sheep getting injured on the way. He slit its throat, then Rebecca and her daughters did the butchering to cut it into smaller pieces. Isaac took the boys scouting for wild herbs, and they cooked the sheep with the herbs for supper over the fire. Beth had a hard time eating it after watching it die. She told herself that it was more honest than buying it from the grocery store, but she still had no appetite for the meat. She ate a few bites, put the rest in her napkin, and threw it out with the plate.

The family sat around the fire in the moonlight after dinner and told stories about this trip up the mountain and all their memories from the trips before. Gus came and leaned against Beth's legs. She patted his head, but it was hard to feel the same about him after he'd eaten all those kittens.

FIRSTBORN

Caleb grabbed Beth's hand and announced, "I want everybody in the family to know we'll be adding another Tucker in just a few months. Beth's pregnant!"

Various shouts of Congratulations! and Hooray! followed. And Samson, the brother closest in age, got up to shake Caleb's hand. Beth smiled with relief. She knew it would be a different story when she finally told her parents.

Rebecca said, "This is a miracle. I was so sad when my baby Gene died after only one month in this world. A grandchild will be a blessing and will help heal our loss."

~~

During the summer, Beth's pregnancy got to the point where hiding it was no longer possible. It was her first summer without any air conditioning and an unusually hot one at that. She'd started wearing low cut jeans and peasant shirts, but no matter what she wore, her clothes stuck to her sweating stomach.

Gail sounded happy when Beth called and asked if she wanted to meet at the Dairy Queen for ice cream. It was a place where they used to hang out, and Beth was dying for ice cream.

Gail looked worried when Beth told her she was pregnant. "You're not going to deliver out there are you?" she asked as she licked her cone.

"I don't know. I haven't decided yet," Beth said. She couldn't believe how good the ice cream tasted. The freezers were so stuffed full of meat, there was no such thing as ice cream at the Tucker ranch.

"I watched my mother have Ben when I was little, and I still remember how painful it looked. At least in the hospital, you'd have medicine if you needed it. Caleb may want you to have the baby out there, but he's not the one who has to do it. You are."

"I'll think about it," Beth promised Gail and headed to her house to see her parents. The driveway and front garden looked so pretty and well-organized when she drove up. And the one-story, wood paneled house was spotlessly clean inside. It seemed so quiet and cool with the air conditioning instead of the noisy fans in the trailer. Her parents met her at the door with big hugs. She could tell they both noticed her stomach.

Her parents weren't surprised when she told them, so it wasn't as bad as she had expected. But when Beth admitted she hadn't seen a doctor yet, they went ballistic.

"No way," said her father, jumping up from the couch.

Her mother said, "Beth, pregnancy can be really dangerous if you don't know what's going on. You have to see a doctor. I don't want you to take any chances."

Beth said, "Everything feels fine to me."

"But you don't know for sure. In the old days, lots of women and babies died during birth without doctors. And I heard it took hours for Isaac to pull that last baby out. I can't imagine how much pain Rebecca was in," her mother said.

FIRSTBORN

Her father said, "Honey, Isaac has no experience compared to a real doctor. You see what happened the last time—the baby died. You should get better medical treatment than a cow."

Beth told her parents she would think about it just like she told Gail. She was being totally truthful because the baby's delivery was all she'd been thinking about lately. She didn't know how to tell Caleb she was too frightened to see what God had in store for her on the Tucker kitchen table, especially when, as far as she was concerned, there was good help right in town.

A month before she thought she might be due to deliver, Beth didn't feel the baby move for an entire morning. She decided to drive the hospital to make sure everything was okay. She knew Caleb was out in the fields and wouldn't miss her. Nor would anyone else around the ranch since she was so useless with most of the chores.

When Beth heard the baby's heartbeat on the monitor, she couldn't stop crying. The nurse ran down the list of routine questions and was alarmed that Beth didn't have a doctor. When Beth said the words *Church of the Firstborn*, the nurse gave a nod of resignation and asked, "Would you mind having a doctor look things over? It would be a lot safer for both of you."

Beth said that she'd be more than happy to have that happen, but she had to be home by five so no one would know about the visit. The nurse said she would do her best to find a doctor who could come right away.

By the time Beth returned to the ranch at five, she'd had all the routine pregnancy bloodwork, an ultrasound, and a pelvic exam. She now knew lots of things that she hadn't known before. She knew that the baby was healthy, that it was probably due on the date she'd figured, that it was a boy, and that his head was not at the bottom of her stomach as it should be, but he was in the flipped around breech position.

That night after dinner, Beth sat at the tiny kitchen table in the trailer peeling the loose strips of orange linoleum off the side and wondering what to say to Caleb. When she heard him come out of the bathroom, she said, "I need to tell you something."

He came in and sat down, worried it was bad news.

She said, "Everything's okay, but I went to the ER today because I was worried. The baby stopped moving and I panicked."

"Why didn't you come and get me?" he asked.

"It didn't seem safe to walk that far if something was really wrong. I was so relieved when they said the baby looked healthy. It's a boy."

His eyes teared up.

"There's one other thing," she said, "The baby is bottom first and the doctor doesn't think it's safe for me to deliver at home."

Caleb said, "The doctor was going to tell you it wasn't safe whatever happened. That's why we don't see doctors in this family."

"I know," Beth said, "but while I was waiting, I called my mom. She and my dad agreed with the doctor, and they're my family too."

Caleb looked stunned. He said, "We have our babies at home around here."

Beth said, "I'm sorry but I've made up my mind. I'm scheduled for a C-section next week,"

"Unlike those fancy doctors in town, my father can actually deliver a breech. He's done it plenty of times with the sheep, and it'll save you an operation," Caleb said.

Beth stuck to her guns and won the argument around midnight.

Caleb was in the operating room for the delivery. Despite his previous objections, the scrubs, mask, and gloves really seemed to suit him. He watched the surgery with interest and was proud to help the pediatrician cut the umbilical cord to its proper length when the baby was in the bassinet.

The baby boy was beautiful, and they named him Daniel. He had Beth's full mouth, Caleb's dark hair, and eyes so dark they were almost black. Caleb was the only Tucker who was ever at the hospital, but Beth's parents were there every day. It was the most time they'd ever spent with Caleb. The three of them were polite to each other but they didn't have much to say.

Since the birth happened right before Thanksgiving, Beth decided to take the rest of the school year off and restart after the Christmas break. When she got back to the trailer from the hospital, she missed her mom's help and everything the nurses did for her. It turned out she had no better luck getting milk out of her own breasts than she had with milking the cow.

When Rebecca saw little Daniel, she told Beth that she was astonished at how much he looked like Gene, the baby she lost. The Tucker family passed him through nine sets of arms when Beth brought him home.

Rebecca was disappointed when she found out Beth was bottle-feeding. And she was adamant that Beth use only natural remedies for pain, so she'd be sure to wake up when Daniel cried at night. Isaac found cause to mention that babies belonged in cribs, not in bed with their parents like he'd heard some lazy young people had them now.

Daniel was always hungry, so Beth trod back and forth to the kitchen all night to warm the bottle then feed him. Her incision hurt worse with every step, and she wondered if it was ever going to get better. Occasionally, she took Extra Strength Tylenol in defiance.

Since the baby didn't have a fixed schedule, no one else did either. Beth's catch-up sleep often happened around the time Caleb woke up, so he started having breakfast with his family in the main house. The trailer refrigerator was almost empty since Beth wasn't able to drive to town to get food. And Caleb was only interested in playing with Daniel and left all the work to her. She often wished he'd feel sorry for her and give her a hand, even if his old-fashioned religion said it was 'women's work'.

Rebecca was too busy to be able to help Beth in the trailer during the day, but she said that Beth could always bring the baby to their house when she was tired. Beth wanted to be as self-reliant as the rest of the Tuckers, so she didn't ask for any help.

The trailer was poorly insulated, and the wind blew through it in the winter. One day when Beth was feeding Daniel, she looked up from their pile of blankets and saw a three-legged cat looking for food. She grabbed a piece of cheese and called to it from the door. It sprung up the steps and came right inside.

She wondered if one kitten had escaped after Gus had only eaten a back leg. The cat finished off two slices of cheese, settled itself in the blankets, and purred when she rubbed its ears. When Caleb got back from feeding the cows, she told him the cat would help get rid of some of the mice in the trailer. Caleb said, "That cat couldn't catch a mouse if it tried."

The cat caught so many mice during the day that Beth lined them up on paper towels to show Caleb when he got home. He said a three-legged cat should still be put down, and Beth was just wasting cat food. One of the reasons she loved Caleb was his quiet competence around animals. She hadn't known it also included cruelty. The cat was gaining weight so fast Beth wondered if she might be pregnant. She pitied her if she was.

As soon as she could drive again, Beth took Daniel to town to spend a day with her mother. There was a fire in the wood stove, and the smell of coffee cake in the air made it feel like heaven. The kitchen seemed huge to her now compared with the one in the trailer. It had so many cabinets and full-size appliances. She sat down in her old chair and dug into the coffee cake at the big wooden table.

Her mother fussed over Daniel and encouraged Beth to take the day off. She spent most of the day in her room looking at old photographs and sleeping. She'd never noticed how comfortable her bed was before. She pulled the quilt up, snuggled down into her pillows, and was happy to have nothing else to do.

When Beth went back to school, Rebecca volunteered to take care of Daniel while she was away. Sitting in classes seemed hard at first because Beth missed both the baby and the cat and the naps they took together. Seeing Gail again cheered her up, but when Gail talked about things like football games and parties, it seemed like another world to Beth. She wondered, even more than before, what relevance school could possibly have to real life.

As time went on, Rebecca became more and more attached to Daniel and earnestly believed he was the reincarnation of little Gene. When Beth mentioned to Caleb that his mother's belief seemed strange, he said, "Reincarnation is one of the main things we believe with our religion. Having faith in God's healing and staying away from doctors is another. And we always give birth at home, no matter what."

"I guess I failed you on the last two," Beth said.

Caleb said, "We weren't surprised since you weren't raised as one of us."

FIRSTBORN

~~

Getting the ditch ready to start irrigating the fields in the spring was such a big event that Beth took a few days off school in March to help. Everything was as beautiful as her first spring in the canyon. The same trees bloomed by the main house, and the sky was the same brilliant blue. She felt different though. Her childhood innocence was long gone, and she knew it would never come back.

As numerous as the Tuckers were, they still needed extra help for burning the ditches after the winter to get rid of any growth that might slow down the water. They needed enough men to form three crews: two men in front with propane torches to set the fires, a few behind them with equipment to stop any fire that got out of control, and a clean-up crew in the rear to remove all the burnt debris. The women were generally left to run messages back and forth since the work was so rough.

At the break of dawn, four Navajo men, who helped burn ditch for all the ranchers up and down the canyon, showed up. They tested the propane torches to make sure they had enough fuel and were working well. Caleb went out to get everyone else set up so they could finish before noon when the wind usually started blowing.

Beth left Daniel with Rebecca after his morning feed and joined them. She found Caleb and his brother Samson walking in the ditch to clear out the charred grasses, and she followed alongside them. There was hardly any wind that morning, so the crew advanced quickly with only a few stray fires to tamp out along the way.

Caleb said to Beth, "Will you go and tell Mama that we'll be ready for lunch around noon? And let her know that the four Navajo want to stick around since they like her food." The two Navajo on his crew turned around and gave him a thumbs up.

Beth walked quickly and was happy to feel useful. She was almost to the house when she heard the screams. She ran back to the field and saw Caleb thrashing on his back with convulsions. Samson was trying to hold him down and move any dangerous equipment out of the way.

"What happened!" she screamed.

"He just ate a bite of one of them wild carrots Daddy showed us growing up at sheep camp last time we were there." Samson handed her the root.

One of the Navajo men looked at the root and said, "He's going to die."

"No, he can't die! cried Beth, stuffing the root into her pocket. "Try to get him as close to the road as you can. I'm going to run and call an ambulance."

The hospital said that it would take at least thirty minutes to get an ambulance there, since the ranch was twenty miles from town. Beth decided to take him instead. She jumped in her car and drove to where the road came closest to the field. Caleb's convulsions were so violent that, in the struggle to get him over the barbed wire fence, everyone got cut up.

FIRSTBORN

The noise from the backseat was unbearable. Caleb thrashed around and screamed out at times, and otherwise moaned like he was in terrible pain. Samson did his best to keep Caleb from hurting himself. "Stay here! Just keep living!" he cried. About halfway to the hospital, Caleb stopped making any sound at all.

Beth asked, "Is he okay? Is he better?"

There was no answer from the back seat.

"Is he okay?" she pleaded.

Samson sobbed, "I think he's passed."

Beth stopped the car. There was blood everywhere, Samson was crying, and Caleb was pale and totally still. She put her head on his chest and didn't hear his heart beating, like she usually did at night before they went to sleep.

Samson said, "Please take him home. We don't believe in doctors and they can't save him now."

She turned around and drove back to the farm.

When they got back, the whole family came running to the car and cried out in grief when they saw Caleb had died. They carefully lifted his body from the car and took him inside the main house.

No one paid much attention to Beth, so she went inside the trailer. Still in shock, she did a quick search on her phone and identified the root as wild hemlock. It was so dangerous that you shouldn't even touch it. Why would Isaac not have known that? How could he have told his sons it was an edible wild carrot when he had never eaten it? She threw it as far away as she could outside the back of the trailer and washed her hands.

Isaac called the men in the canyon to help him dig a grave and made a simple wooden coffin for the funeral the next day. Rebecca washed the body and dressed Caleb in his best clothes. Beth brought the clothes over to the house from the trailer, but she wasn't able to help. She was so upset that she couldn't bear the thought of seeing Caleb's body another time, even though it might be the last. She cleaned the blood from the inside of her car instead.

She called her parents to let them know what happened. They wanted to come and get her immediately, but she was too exhausted. She told them that the funeral was tomorrow because the body needed to be buried within twenty-four hours in the ranch graveyard. She promised her mother she'd be okay, and she'd see them at the funeral after she got some sleep. But she couldn't sleep.

Daniel stayed overnight with the Tuckers because Beth didn't feel safe taking care of him. She knew it was better for everyone, but she'd never felt so alone. Nothing felt real without Caleb there. When she sat at the trailer kitchen table with its peeling linoleum, it felt like she was in the middle of nowhere. She wondered how she was going to go on with her life without him.

The next day everyone gathered at the lonely corner of the ranch where the Tuckers had always been buried. The older graves had engraved stones with simple names and dates.

The more recent ones, like baby Gene, had only carved pieces of wood because stone had become too costly.

They lowered the wooden box carefully into the grave with ropes. The men in the Tucker family then covered it and packed the soil, while the rest of the family and friends sang *Amazing Grace*. Beth was too upset to sing so she stood in silence. She was surprised when she looked up and saw her parents joining in. Her mother was wearing a dress and her father had on a dark suit. They looked so out of place that it seemed strange they knew the words.

Isaac read a passage from the Bible, then Rebecca spoke.

"Caleb was such a special soul that I'm sure he'll be reincarnated soon, and I hope I'll be able to meet him again before I die. God gave me one miracle when he brought back my baby Gene as baby Daniel, and I give thanks every day when I see his angelic face. I know I shouldn't be asking for so much, but this family has seen its share of tragedy and I know God has mercy. I pray to Jesus that we all see Caleb again before we leave this life. We will all miss him so much."

~~

Afterwards, her parents asked Beth if she'd like to come home for dinner and to spend the night. She went to the trailer to grab some clothes and hugged all the Tuckers before she drove away. She took the cat with her and left Daniel with Rebecca.

Despite her parents urging, she never went back.

LUCKY

The log cabin had been converted into a chapel with a tall arched window behind the altar. Through it, you could see a waterfall cascading down the rocks in the distance and a small meadow covered with white daisies in front. The chapel was overflowing with wildflowers inside; blue lupines, spiky red penstemon, daisies, and sunflowers. The bridesmaids, Maggie and Kate, wore dresses that lit up the room. They were a rich gold color, and the velvet shimmered when they moved.

A flute was playing when Linda walked down the aisle with her father, Ray, who shed a few tears on the way. Her dress was elegant and simple to show off her slim figure, and her veil was made of authentic old lace, which complimented her chestnut hair, big brown eyes, and healthy tan. When Mike came down the aisle, he looked tall and handsome. He was smiling like he couldn't believe his luck.

Linda knew everything was perfect and had good reason to believe she was right. She had worked out the design for the bridesmaid's dresses years ago and had seen the wedding many times in her dreams. She knew it would be in the chapel at Dawson Hot Springs; a ghost town in the high Rockies that had been turned into a stylish resort.

She'd been searching for the perfect man to play the groom since she was fifteen, and it took six years to finally find

Mike. When Maggie and Kate saw his blue eyes and muscles bulging under his tee-shirt, they were immediately jealous. Mike was practical and kind and seemed to adore her. It was an unexpected bonus when he was able to pay for everything too.

Mike's family had been in the irrigation business for three generations, and with all the droughts in the Southwest, plenty of irrigation was needed. The farmers didn't want to waste their allotment of water, so they often sought advice and equipment from the professionals.

Linda had another boyfriend for all four years of high school. Joe was kind and patient, and she'd let him kiss her, but she didn't go all the way like Maggie did. They often talked about the future; the children they would have and what their house would look like. Linda was stunned when Joe suddenly announced he didn't want to get married in his twenties. She broke it off immediately, and he missed the reward he'd been waiting for all those years.

She was sad for a while, but soon afterwards her father was able to afford an irrigation system for their three acres, and Mike appeared. She watched Mike work from her bedroom window and found as many reasons as she could to stroll around outside in tight jeans and halter tops. It paid off in the end, and now she had everything she wanted. Her father had often promised all her dreams would come true.

It had just been the two of them when Linda was growing up. Her mother died in a horse accident when she was only two, and Ray took over both roles and gave her everything she needed. She had a car, a closet full of clothes, and his undivided attention.

Her father had a few girlfriends over the years, but none had been serious until Annabel. Ray met her when he dropped off produce to the Food Bank where she worked. Now she helped Ray with the organic farm and had taken Linda's place at the stall in the Durango Farmer's Market.

The plan was for her to move in when Linda left. Annabel enjoyed selling the vegetables and chatting with strangers and didn't mind when there wasn't much money at the end of the day. She said that a simple life was a Godly one.

~~

Linda and Mike went to Hawaii for their honeymoon and returned to a brand-new house on ten acres in Summit Ridge. Mike had called the contractors several times on the trip to make sure everything would be just right for Linda when they arrived at their new home. She took a selfie to send to Maggie and Kate when he carried her over the threshold and gave him a big hug as soon as he put her down.

Walking from room to room, Linda was kind enough not to mention the things that weren't perfect. The kitchen cabinets he'd selected had paned glass, but they weren't like the ones she'd picked out in the catalogue, and the Jacuzzi wasn't exactly centered in front of the plate glass window with the mountain view as she'd planned. She was happy he'd left choosing the furniture to her, so there would be no more mistakes and the house would look just the way she wanted it to be.

LUCKY

The only furniture in the house was in the bedroom. There were two leather chairs and a TV on one side of the room with a low table in front where they could eat. The king bed loomed large on the other side with its aspen log posts and matching bedside tables.

The reality of life as a couple was just beginning to dawn on Linda. She was surprised at how much time Mike wanted to spend playing around in bed during their trip. No one had warned her about honeymoon cystitis, and she had a serious urinary tract infection by the second day. She was relieved when the doctor recommended temporary abstinence. The infection was so painful she was worried about it happening again before she got home.

When Ray and Annabel came to visit, they were impressed by the four-bedroom house and the ten acres. Ray helped Linda plan where to put the horse pasture and where to build the barn. Linda was afraid of riding since her mother had died in a horse accident, but she did like the way horses looked around a ranch.

For the next few months, Linda worked hard looking through magazines and catalogues. She picked out floral quilts and had all the sheets and towels monogrammed in gold. She found a dining room table with a colorful painting of cowboys rounding up cows covering the entire top of it and bought a huge chandelier made of elk antlers to hang over it. Mike was impressed with everything she did.

He said, "This house looks just like the ones in the magazines. You design homes just as good as you design your outfits. I'm living with a fashion model and an interior designer!"

Linda smiled, "You can pick out some things for the house if you want. It's not through yet." They were admiring the gold initials on the towels in the bathroom.

"No, I like it your way. I can tell how smart you are by watching all this come together." Mike put his arms around Linda and said, "Hey, you want to get in the Jacuzzi?"

She gave him a kiss on the cheek, untangled herself and said, "The doctor says no hanky-panky until I straighten out these infections with the new medicine."

"I sure hope it's soon. It's been two months, and you look so hot I can't wait much longer."

Linda smiled, "Thanks sweetie. He said these things can take a while and need to be left alone until the treatment works."

Mike turned off the Jacuzzi water and playfully patted her behind, "That's okay honey, let's just have dinner. I don't want to mess anything up down there."

~~

The house was finished just in time to have both their families over for Thanksgiving dinner. When Annabel and Ray arrived, Linda took them over to see the new barn and the pasture with two spotted appaloosa horses hanging their heads over the fence. When Mike's parents came, he ran to get the Southern Living magazine to show them how Linda's food table looked just like the one on the cover. He told them she'd been

LUCKY

working for days to cook every single Thanksgiving recipe in the magazine, so dinner was going to be delicious.

Linda had set up two tables under the elk antlers. The food table, with its white tablecloth and silver candlesticks, was almost too small for all the food. There was a ten-pound turkey, cornbread dressing, squash casserole, green beans, rice, cranberries, rolls, gravy, and pecan pies for dessert. Bottles of Pinot Grigio and Shiraz stood proudly in the middle, and pressed autumn leaves were scattered around on the cloth.

The second table was the one with the cowboy painting, which had a glass top to protect it. She had decided not to use a tablecloth or placemats, so everyone could admire the art underneath their plates while they were eating.

Mike's father said, "This table reminds me of the time Mike was trying to practice roping sheep so he could be in the junior part of the rodeo. Our ram knocked that poor kid down and butted him all day long, but Mike didn't want no help. He always wanted to figure out everything on his own. Even when he was four, he'd tell me to get lost."

Mike's mother nodded in agreement. They both looked like they were from another era. His father, Wesley, wore a black shirt and bolo tie and had a big rodeo buckle under his paunch. His mother, Annette, looked equally solid under her loose print dress with its dainty lace collar.

Linda looked across the table at Ray and smiled, "Sounds like Mike is just as macho as you are, Daddy." She glanced around the table and asked, "Who wants to say grace?"

Annabel quickly volunteered. She gave thanks to the Lord for the company, the food, and the beautiful day. At the end, she gave a special thanks to God for helping Ray find his way to Jesus. Everyone clapped, and Ray smiled and said, "Amen!" Linda had never seen her father so happy.

Annabel wore a bright orange dress that almost reached her ankles, and Ray wore a white shirt with a neat row of buttons and a mandarin collar. He was the only one at the table wearing sneakers instead of cowboy boots. Everyone enjoyed each other's company and raved about the food. After they waved goodbye to everybody at the door, Mike turned around to Linda with tears in his eyes and said, "I'm the luckiest guy in the world."

That night, they had sex for the first time in quite a while, but it burned afterwards. It took Linda another month of treatment before she felt like things were back in order.

~~

When there was a thick cover of snow on the ground that winter, Linda made plans to go snowmobiling with her father on Dawson Mountain. There was nothing Ray liked better than speeding across acres of pristine snow in the Rocky Mountains, and he'd started letting Linda ride in front of him when she was only two.

Mike had a snowmobile he hadn't used in years and was eager to come along on the Saturday they had in mind. Linda and Ray decided to drive up together, like old times, and have Mike follow along behind them.

LUCKY

It was snowing on the day they'd planned, but not enough to cancel the trip. With the three snowmobiles in tow, they made slow progress on the narrow road that led to the hot springs. When the trucks finally turned through the gate and drove over the bridge into Dawson Hot Springs, Linda and her father saw a starving coyote lying in the snow on the bank above the river.

Linda told Mike about it as soon as they parked the trucks, and they all walked back to the riverbank together. The animal was so weak that it didn't move when they were only a few feet away.

Mike had a heavy old blanket in his pickup. When they threw it around the coyote, it still didn't move a muscle. The two men held the edges of the blanket together to protect themselves, but the coyote didn't fight or snarl as they carried it back to Ray's truck. They noticed it was a female when they put her in the back seat. Ray turned on the heat, and she quickly fell asleep.

The resort was closed for the winter, but Mike knew Keith, the manager. They walked over to his cabin, and he asked them inside. Keith was soft spoken with deep weather creases in his face. He had a big fire in the wood burning stove and a bowl of oatmeal on the table in front of it.

Mike said, "We found a starving coyote pup in the snow by the river. Have you seen one hanging around here?"

"No, I haven't even seen animal tracks the past month or so. Almost all the animals move down when the snow's this deep. Where's it now?" Keith asked.

Ray said, "We have her in our truck."

Keith put on a heavy coat and walked over with them to see her. They watched her through the windows of the truck. She was still asleep, and her breathing seemed regular. When they opened the door, she opened her eyes and looked at them calmly.

Keith went back to his cabin to get some turkey sausage he had in the refrigerator. He handed it to her wearing a thick canvas glove. She ate all of it and put her head back down to sleep, so they closed the door of the truck to keep the heat in.

Mike said, "We came up here to go snowmobiling. What should we do with her?"

Keith glanced back toward his cabin, "I don't know. I have two cats inside so I can't keep her here. She'd eat them both in no time flat."

"We can take her to our place," Linda said, "Let's go snowmobiling for a little while and then we'll take her back down and see what happens."

Mike said, "She's a wild animal. All sorts of things could happen!" His bright blue eyes were his prominent feature, and they opened even wider whenever he was alarmed.

"She's also a dog," Linda said, "Please Mike please. Let's give it a try. We can always take her to the wildlife refuge if things go wrong." She looked through the window at the coyote sleeping quietly.

Keith said, "I can check on her while you're up there. She should be okay with some food in her stomach, and it'll be a lot warmer with that blanket in the truck than lying in the snow."

Ray said, "Good plan. Let's get going!" He gave Keith a pat on the back and told him they'd be back before too long.

Linda sent photos of the coyote to Maggie and Kate while the boys unloaded the snowmobiles. She decided to name her Lucky.

The snow was surprisingly deep. As soon as they stepped off the packed areas, they were sunk in snow up to their knees and still couldn't feel the bottom. Fortunately, the snowmobiles carved through the snow with no problem. Ray and Linda took the lead since they knew the road to the high meadows.

When they got to the top, it started snowing harder so Ray decided to speed up to see as many of his favorite places as possible. They passed by an old one-room log cabin with big wooden snowshoes hanging beside the door, then went farther afield to look across a deep ravine with a row of saw-toothed mountains standing like granite soldiers on the other side. On the way back, they circled around to the old silver mine and took care to avoid the rusted equipment sticking out of the snow.

Mike's snowmobile was an older model, and the more it snowed, the more trouble he had keeping up with the others. And the more distance between the snowmobiles, the harder Linda and Ray's tracks were to follow. He revved it up as much as he could.

After the mine, he watched them disappear around a narrow bend, and as he rounded it behind them, he felt himself sliding off to the side. He jumped away from the machine, as it quickly hurtled down the hundred-foot embankment and rolled over rocks and bumped through trees until he got to the bottom. He lay motionless and still in the deep snow for a while trying to catch his breath, then decided to try to get up. He moved cautiously and checked each limb for broken bones before bearing down with any weight.

It was ten minutes before Ray and Linda realized Mike wasn't behind them. By the time they turned around to look for him, the snow had picked up considerably and his tracks were covered. "Linda! Ray!" Mike yelled from the bottom when he heard them pass, but they couldn't hear him over the loud engines. When he realized they hadn't slowed down, Mike yelled out in frustration.

He sat on a tree for a few minutes hoping they would turn around and look for him again, but lost hope in the snowy silence. He tried to climb up the steep bank but slipped and fell losing ground each time he made progress.

When they saw no sign of Mike on the road, Linda and Ray decided he must have gone back down the mountain because of the heavy snow. It was getting darker by the minute, and with the snow flying, they had to concentrate to stay on the trail. They pulled in behind the trucks then got off and looked around but didn't see Mike's snowmobile anywhere at the bottom. Linda opened the door of Ray's truck and looked inside to check on Lucky. The coyote was shivering and barely opened her eyes.

Keith's lights were on, so they knocked on his door. When he saw only two of them standing on the porch, he looked alarmed. He asked, "Where's Mike?"

Linda said, "We don't know. We thought he was down here."

After they explained to Keith what had happened, he said, "Mike must still be on the mountain in all this snow. We need to get the rescue crews out."

Linda said, "Let's wait a little. He might've decided to look around somewhere up there and be on his way back right now. He'd be upset if you called for help and he didn't need it."

Ray said, "I agree. I think he'd be real embarrassed if we called Search & Rescue for nothing."

Linda asked, "What's going on with Lucky? She looks awful."

Keith said, "Lucky? You mean the coyote? I'd say she's not doing too well. She's refusing to eat more food and won't drink any water. I'm not sure she's going to make it."

Linda teared up. She said, "We've got to get on the road right now and take her home to see if we can save her life. We shouldn't have stayed out so long. I'm sure Mike will stop by here when he comes back. Just let him know it was an emergency and we had to leave." She headed for the door.

Ray ran to catch up with Linda and called back to Keith, "Thanks for all your help! Let us know what happens."

Keith threw on his warmest gear, grabbed a flashlight, and ran outside to his snowmobile. Linda and Ray saw it climbing the hill in the thick of the snowstorm as they drove away.

~~

Linda decided to stay in her old bedroom at her father's place overnight because there was a good place for Lucky to sleep in his basement. The roads were deep in snow on the way back, so the going was slow. Linda kept checking the backseat to make sure Lucky was alive and asking Ray to drive faster. Finally arriving at Ray and Annabel's house, they carried Lucky limp in their arms inside and down the stairs.

Linda checked her cellphone in the kitchen and was surprised that Keith hadn't left a message to say Mike was back and all was well. She felt in her heart that Mike was okay, and she trusted her intuition. She tried to call both Keith and Mike, but neither of them answered.

Annabel put newspapers on the floor and made Lucky a bed in a warm corner with towels and blankets, and Ray put up an old, but sturdy, child's gate and brought down a big bowl of water. Linda offered Lucky some hunks of meat barehanded, and the coyote raised her head and ate a little. She'd become so thin that her ears were now her dominant feature. Annabel said she looked like a fruit bat, and Ray guessed she was around eight months old.

LUCKY

Another hour passed without any word from Keith. Annabel looked out the basement window at the streetlight and saw the snowflakes pouring down around it. She said, "Let's have a prayer meeting and ask for the Lord's help to get Mike home safely."

Ray looked up from the TV and said, "At this point, I guess it's all we can do. I feel terrible about not helping Keith. We left so quickly I didn't even get to tell him what trails we took. It's the least I could have done."

Linda got up from the blanket she was lying on right outside Lucky's gate, "I'm sorry Daddy. I figured Mike was going to be okay, and Lucky looked like she was going to die. You think she'll be okay if we leave her down here alone?"

Ray got up from the recliner and said, "She probably needs sleep as much as anything else. Let's go upstairs to pray. We can try to feed her some more meat afterwards."

Upstairs, Annabel dimmed the lights, and they sat at the small kitchen table and joined hands. They all closed their eyes and Annabel led them in a prayer. Linda had never prayed anywhere but in a church. She was reminded of spooky seances she'd had with her preteen friends.

It wasn't until the morning that they got a call from Keith. He said the rescue team had finally found Mike when the sun came up. He'd had an accident on the snowmobile near the silver mine and climbed up a hundred feet to get back to the trail. He was on his hands and knees when they found him, bloody and freezing, trying to make it down the trail so he could find his way back to Dawson Hot Springs.

Keith said, "I'm with Mike right now in the hospital. He's getting treatment for hypothermia."

Linda said, "We're on our way."

"I have to warn you he's not making a whole lot of sense right now. He's going over and over what happened and keeps asking me why you and Ray didn't stop when he had the accident and why you left him on the mountain in a snowstorm. He can't believe you went all the way back home and didn't wait to make sure he was okay."

Linda said, "We didn't know he had an accident. All we knew was he wasn't behind us anymore. And we were worried! We had a prayer meeting for him here at the house. We couldn't have done anything to help Mike if we'd stayed around, and Lucky wouldn't have made it unless we came back."

Ray and Linda threw on some clothes and sped to the hospital. Linda rushed into Mike's room and gave him a dramatic hug. A tear ran down his cheek. Mike was silent as they stood by the bed, and after a while, he said he was tired and wanted to go to sleep. Linda took a photo, and sent it out to everyone she knew, with a caption that read, "My brave husband survived the snowstorm on Dawson Mountain!"

Two days later, Mike was discharged from the hospital. By that time, Lucky was eating well and able to stand up and walk around a little. Mike was weak but had no physical injuries aside from cuts and bruises. Linda fussed over Mike the first week. She even took off her clothes and got in bed beside

LUCKY

him one night, but he said he was too exhausted. By the second week she was tired of his sullen behavior.

Lucky was grateful for all the attention Linda gave her. She stood up every time she heard Linda's footsteps and eagerly ate any food she was given. She seemed comfortable when Linda sat on the floor near her and had even let her touch her ears. Her eyes looked bright and hopeful.

When Mike went back to work, Linda asked Ray to come over and help her figure out how to redesign the mud room so Lucky could live in half of it and have her own dog door. She also wanted to build an outside pen that was strong enough so the coyote wouldn't be able to escape. Mike made the calls and oversaw the construction just to be done with the smell of soiled newspapers.

Lucky liked being outdoors and slept in the snow most nights, leaving her stack of blankets inside untouched. Linda managed to slip a collar around her neck, but she growled and fought when she was being pulled by a leash, so Linda bought a big dog kennel for transport instead.

Lucky was much less comfortable around Mike. She followed all his movements with worried eyes whenever he was near her enclosure. One Saturday in the early spring, Linda wanted to get a picture of the two of them together before he left to go turkey hunting.

She blocked the dog door so Lucky wouldn't hide inside, but when Mike walked into her pen, she still ran over to huddle in the far corner next to the fence.

Linda couldn't get both of them in the frame on her phone. She said, "Can't you get a little closer? Maybe she's afraid of your gun."

Mike said, "There's no way she knows about guns. Besides, I'm glad she's afraid of me. It shows she has some sense. You should've never have handled her as much as you did. She needs to be afraid of people or she's going to get killed by the first stranger she walks up to."

Linda put her hand through the fence and stroked the coyote's ears, "I couldn't help it. She's always loved me because she knows I saved her life."

Mike let himself out of the gate and said, "We got pictures of you and Lucky all over the place. You don't need one of me."

Linda watched him drive off in the truck and wondered why he always spoiled everything she thought was special.

~~

One afternoon in mid-April, Linda found Lucky trying to climb the eight-foot fence to escape, so they installed a shock wire at the top. The snowmelt was running fast in the creek at the bottom, and the blackjack oaks and aspens were budding with bright green leaves. Linda felt guilty the coyote wouldn't be able to run through the fields and drink the fresh water. Since she wasn't even able to take her out for a walk, Lucky might as well be in prison.

A few nights later, Mike and Linda were startled awake at midnight by a chorus of eerie coyote yips and howls right outside their door. Linda tiptoed around to the mudroom in her robe and heard Lucky barking and howling at full volume to answer the other coyotes. Linda was thankful they'd installed the shock wire so Lucky wouldn't be able to get out and the wild coyotes wouldn't be able to get in.

When Mike dressed and went outside, it was so dark with the new moon that he couldn't see anything at all. The sound was coming from the direction of the creek, but he could tell the coyotes were much closer. After the waves of howling continued for another ten minutes, he went inside to get his gun.

Linda saw him round the corner with the gun and said, "Mike please don't shoot them. They're only here because of Lucky. They don't mean us any harm."

Mike grumbled, "It's so dark out there I couldn't shoot them if I tried. I'm going to fire up in the air and see if that'll quieten them down."

After the gunshot, the pack stopped yipping for two minutes, but started back up as soon as Mike went inside and closed the door. He tried firing a few more times then gave up. Mike and Linda got back in bed and piled the pillows over their heads, but it was impossible to sleep. The coyotes didn't leave until the light of dawn seeped in around the curtains.

Linda got up to check on Lucky as soon as it was daylight and found her outside staring at the creek bottom. She didn't respond when Linda called her name and was startled when Linda stroked her ears. When Lucky came in to eat, there was a small, dark stain on the floor where she'd been sitting. Linda knew it meant she was in heat; the vet had warned her it was going to happen soon.

The coyotes continued to howl outside Lucky's cage every night until sunrise. Lucky yipped along, Mike started going to bed as soon as he'd finished dinner, and Linda tried to nap during the day.

After the fifth sleepless night, Mike said, "Honey, we've got to do something about this." They were bending over their blue and yellow sunflower coffee mugs at the kitchen table.

Linda rested her head on her hand, "Lucky's bound to stop being in heat any day now. Then things will be back to normal."

Mike said, "Only until she goes into heat again. You saved her life, now you've got to let her go. She's a wild animal, not a dog you can keep."

Linda teared up, "But you said if we let her go, somebody's going to shoot her if she's friendly to them." She wondered if he wanted to get rid of Lucky because he still held a grudge against both of them after the accident.

"If we release her into a coyote pack up on the mountain, she'll never see anybody up there to be friendly to," Mike said.

"How do you know the coyotes in the pack won't kill her when she walks up?"

"I'll have my gun with me, and I'll shoot any one of them that attacks her. I really don't think they will." He got up, poured himself a bowl of Cheerios, and sat back down to eat it.

Linda put her hand over her eyes, "I would miss her so much if she was gone!"

Mike looked at her from across the table, "Linda, we said we wanted to have kids. We can't trust Lucky to be safe around a child. There was a report of a coyote attacking a child in California just last week. We can get a dog to replace her."

Linda looked up with defiance and said, "No ordinary dog would ever replace her. She's beautiful and wild just like me." Mike shook his head. He didn't know what she meant. What made her think that she, of all people, was wild? He sighed and went out to his truck to leave for work.

When he came home that afternoon, he could tell she was still upset. Usually they discussed what to eat for dinner, but instead, she disappeared to the bedroom. He heated a frozen pizza, made a salad, and poured beer into their favorite mugs. When she didn't appear, he brought her dinner in bed and finally convinced her there was no other solution but his plan.

The more she thought about it, the sadder Linda felt. Mike was worried that her anxiety about losing Lucky would get worse the longer he waited. He was also afraid she would change her mind.

He called Keith to find out if he'd seen coyotes on the mountain now that the snowmelt had started. Keith said he'd driven by a pack of them hanging around a deer carcass near the old silver mine at dusk. He agreed with Mike that releasing Lucky near the place they'd found her was the only thing that made sense.

When Mike told Linda that he planned to take Lucky back up to the mountain in two days, she left the kitchen table in the middle of breakfast. He heard her call her father and ask if she could come home to sleep in her old bedroom until everything was over. Mike was shocked when she packed quickly and left without saying goodbye. After five minutes of silence, he realized it was a relief.

On Saturday morning, Mike met a friend in town at the El Grande Café and had steak and eggs for breakfast. They sat in the booth's old Naugahyde seats and discussed the best way to release the coyote.

He got back home around noon. The house looked like an abandoned spaceship since there were no bushes or trees planted around it yet. He gave the horses a slice of hay, made sure they had enough water, and walked back over to the house.

Lucky came out to the fence and followed alongside him when he got closer. He knew it meant she was hungry because he'd left without feeding her breakfast. Linda was always able to lead Lucky into the kennel by holding her collar, but Mike planned to lure her in with food. He carried the kennel into her pen, put a good portion of hamburger meat in the back of it, and stood off to one side. As soon as she went in to eat, he moved fast and closed the kennel door.

LUCKY

He picked up his gun and took it to the truck, then gently slid the kennel onto the back seat. Lucky cried when he started the truck but quieted down as soon as they got on the road.

The trip to Dawson Mountain took about two hours, and by the time they got there it was almost dusk. On the way to the silver mine, he stopped by the place where he'd had the snowmobile accident and couldn't even see down to the bottom, it was so steep.

He drove slowly once he was near the place where Keith told him the carcass was located and stopped the truck two hundred feet short when he saw it. He slid the kennel off the back seat and put it halfway between the truck and the hulk of rib bones and pelts of fur, which were all that was left of the deer. He got back in the truck to wait.

After an hour or so, a few coyotes appeared. They were cautious at first but became more comfortable as time passed. One of them went over to sniff the kennel, but there was no sound from Lucky inside. They scattered when Mike quietly eased himself out of the truck. He went to the kennel, opened the door, then ran to hide in the brush. He raised his gun and waited.

Lucky stayed in the kennel for a few minutes and then cautiously stepped out. By that time, the other coyotes had reappeared. The moment she saw them, she turned and ran towards Mike. His shot rang through the air. She fell, shuddered, and lay still.

TOUGH ENOUGH: TEN STORIES

Mike wiped his hands on his jeans and walked over to where she lay. His shot had hit her right through the chest, so she'd died quickly. He shook his head and picked up the empty dog kennel. It bounced when he put it on the backseat. He slid his gun in the rack, turned the truck around, and unwrapped a piece of chewing gum for his ride back down the mountain.

THREE BULLFIGHTS

~ I ~

They were staying in southern Spain for a month in a small stone house perched over a deep gorge. The house in Ronda was owned by Christopher, her husband's friend, who couldn't tolerate the heat and was never there in summer. Holly liked to walk to the edge of the slate patio and watch the small black silhouettes of cows moving in the fields at the bottom.

In the evenings, they went to a bar across the street to drink sherry and eat ham and olives. At the end of the night, they finished with brandy and ripe oranges. Holly slept well and didn't stir until the old-fashioned church bells began to ring in the morning.

She had been married to William for only a year, and she was already a character in two of his stories. She knew he was thinking of her whenever he described a tanned woman with beautiful hands and blonde hair streaked from the sun.

Since working reception at the art gallery, she'd dreamt of inspiring an artist and becoming his muse. Holly had graduated from Berkley with a major in art history and admired the artists that came to the gallery and appreciated their work.

She was twenty-six when they met in San Francisco. William was ten years older and had traveled the world. She went to a reading of his novel about the California gold rush called *All the Gold in the Sunset*. She asked him to autograph a book, and he asked her to dinner. It wasn't long before she'd moved into his apartment in Pacific Heights.

There were other women in his life, but she set aside any doubts when he asked her to marry him one month later. She loved him and wanted to make his adventurous life even better by looking after all the details. They dreamt of a house in Sonoma one day.

~~

She enjoyed the morning sun in Spain, so she moved one of Christopher's tables outside to the patio and covered it with a lace tablecloth she'd found in an antique store down the street. She bought strong coffee, bread, onions, eggs, and potatoes from the market. They ate breakfast outside, before the heat set in, when the air rising from the gorge still felt cool and delicious. At night, they sat at the table in the dark, and she pointed out the constellations.

William rented a car, and they drove down to the coast, where they found a restaurant overlooking the city of Malaga. William's Spanish was good, but Holly's was better. She charmed the waiter as soon as they walked in the door. He brought them free dishes of wild asparagus, fresh sardines, squid in ink, and spicy shrimp. The table was covered in empty terracotta plates when they were through.

The waiter bowed in Holly's direction at the end of the meal and asked, "*Les disfrutaron de la comida?*"

THREE BULLFIGHTS

Holly said, "*Todo estuvo delicioso.*"

He turned to William and said, "*Su marida es muy encantadora.*"

William smiled at Holly and said, "I know."

After the brief trip to busy Malaga, they were grateful to return to the house in Ronda, a much less touristy town. Christopher's original welcome note explained that the town was a well-kept secret, known primarily for having the oldest bullring in Spain. He recommended the Bullfighters Museum, so they went one afternoon. There were life-sized bronze statues of men roping a heavily muscled bull near the entrance.

William had been to several bullfights in the past and relished his memories of them. Holly knew there was still bullfighting in Spain in 1980, but she preferred her childhood notion of *Ferdinand the Bull*, who "liked to sit quietly under a tree and smell the flowers".

The museum walls were covered in colorful posters from famous fights in the past as well as old photographs. The circular museum was styled as an imitation bullring with arches painted on the inside walls and cheering crowds painted in the stadium behind them. Holly found the photographs disturbing, but she acted interested and asked questions.

"I didn't know the matadors were lifted up off the ground by the bulls when they're gored. Is that what happens?" she asked.

"Yes. You can see how the matador is holding onto the bull's horn to stabilize his body and keep the horn from ripping through internal organs. It doesn't always work, and I remember that matador dying after the fight." William pronounced the name to himself.

Holly moved across the room and saw another photograph that made her catch her breath. She called William over to look at it.

She asked, "The horse lying on his side bleeding in this picture, don't they have protection?"

"The horses have a protective cape, but the bulls can get underneath them and gore their stomachs."

William paused in front of the next picture. "The banderilleros are very brave, usually matadors in training. They don't have horses like the picadors do. They stab these barbed darts in the bull's shoulder on foot to make him angry enough to fight." He pointed to the brightly colored banderillas in the bull's shoulder. What Holly saw were the thick streams of blood running down from where the flags were planted.

On the way out, William noticed a new poster near the ticket office, "Look! There's a bullfight in a town that's close to us this weekend. We can go."

Holly nodded but didn't smile. William was already too busy buying the tickets to notice.

The day of the bullfight was particularly hot. They stopped before the town beside a grassy field to eat a picnic of sardines and fresh fruit Holly had put together. There were so many flies it was impossible to eat without getting one in your mouth, and a cloud of them got into the car.

THREE BULLFIGHTS

The traditional town fair before the bullfight was already in full swing when they arrived. There were big tents with banners on them, and throngs of people milling around between them. Through the open tent flaps, they could see food, musicians, and flamenco dancing inside.

One of the tents was for the Spanish Socialist Workers Party. It intrigued Holly because her father often played an album of songs from the Spanish Civil War. He was a welder for a metal fabrication plant in New Mexico where she grew up and a staunch member of the workers union. They went inside to see if she recognized any of the music.

After only a few minutes, a well-dressed older gentleman, who introduced himself as Señor Guzmán, spotted them and came in to ask where they were from. After some preliminary conversation, he said, "You're too good-looking a couple to be in this tent. I'll take you to one with better dancers and delicious food."

William followed with Holly trailing behind. Señor Guzmán's tent had *Centro Democratico* on the banner, and the flamenco dancing was forceful and dramatic. William was pleased to have found a better tent, but Holly felt sorry they had left the Socialist tent despite its relative poverty.

Their distinguished new companion introduced them to several members of his family and also mentioned that he was the mayor of the town. Before Holly knew it, William had agreed to have lunch at the family home before the bullfight and they were following behind them in the car. William had drunk quite a few glasses of red wine at the tent, but his driving seemed okay.

As soon as they walked in Señor Guzmán's house, he proudly showed them pictures on the walls of himself with Generalissimo Franco—leader of the fascists during the Spanish Civil War and dictator afterwards until 1975. Holly sent silent apologies to her father in New Mexico for even stepping foot in the place.

Lunch was brought by several servants to a table beside a swimming pool in the courtyard. A male turkey wandered by with his chest puffed out and tail feathers in full array. Holly excused herself to look at him more closely. A gardener, with jangling keyrings attached to his belt loops, walked over from the pool and asked if she liked the *pavo macho*. She said he was *muy impresionante*.

When they returned to their car to leave for the bullfight, they found the turkey standing in the passenger seat. They told the gardener they had no place to keep the *pavo macho*, and with a sad face, he removed it and waved goodbye.

The bullring was not far from the mayor's house. When everyone arrived, the family insisted Holly and William should exchange their tickets for better ones next to them in the VIP area. After William gave the mayor the tickets to exchange, he and Holly waited outside.

They wandered over to the outside paddock where the horses were kept before the bullfight. A white gelding in a tattered cape came over to the railing and stood close to them.

THREE BULLFIGHTS

William said, "Look at that old soldier. I bet he's been through the wars. See all those scars on his stomach?"

Holly said, "With the cape covering his head, how can he even see the bull coming?"

"They'd run if they saw the bull coming so they drug them, stuff their ears, and blindfold them. I've heard they even cut the vocal cords, so their screams don't upset the crowd." William seemed unfazed by what he was saying.

"How could that be okay?" Holly asked. She felt sick to her stomach imagining it.

"They use horses destined for the glue factory who are sent there to be destroyed. At least they get to live a little longer."

"I guess that's some small mercy," Holly said. What she didn't say was that death at the glue factory seemed preferable to torture.

On the way to the seats Holly put herself last in line and sat next to William on the far side of the family, who sent many smiles her way. She was relieved the VIP seats weren't the ones closest to the bottom because she wanted to be as far away as possible from the action. She planned not to watch the fight unless she had to. It didn't work for long.

William said, "These are the picadors."

She looked up and saw two men with lances riding those poor blinded, deafened, silenced horses with inadequate protection.

"They put those lances in the bull's shoulder to weaken the neck muscles so he can't raise his head." Holly wanted to know less, not more, about what was going on, but she didn't want to ruin the event for William.

When the matador made a dramatic entrance to begin the fight, William grabbed her hand, smiled, and held it tightly so she felt compelled to watch what was happening. Holly winced when the matador moved in for the kill, but the sword didn't go deep enough and bounced off the bull's back. It took many blood spattering attempts before he finally sank it between the shoulder blades.

William said, "That was a very poor kill."

Holly was silent as she watched a man jump on the bull's back to saw off the ears while another sawed off the tail. They rode around the ring proudly displaying the bull's body parts when they were through.

"Let's hope the other bullfighters are better," William added.

"Other bullfighters?" Holly now realized it was a lot of fanfare for a twenty-minute spectacle. There were bound to be more bullfights.

"Yes, there are five more bulls, so you should get to see a clean kill. These bulls don't go to waste. It's considered an honor to eat the meat, though I've heard the stress on the bull makes it hard to chew."

As it happened, there were no clean kills that day. They said goodbye to the family at the arena and politely turned down their offer to stay for the night. On the way home, Holly told William that she didn't want to go to another bullfight.

William said, "It'll grow on you. My first one was rough too."

They spent the last week of their trip exploring the hill towns around Ronda where old men sat and gossiped in the town squares. Holly had one sleepless night after the bullfight then returned to her usual pattern. She was able to sleep well and wake with the church bells in the morning, but she looked forward to getting back to a culture she could understand.

~ II ~

The hills near their new house in California reminded Holly of the ones in Spain. They were covered in the same feathery yellow grass with scattered gnarled oaks and the occasional dry creek bed. The air felt similar too with a spicy dried tobacco smell. They'd been in the house for four years. Holly had a north facing studio in the back and was trying her hand at painting.

She liked to walk in the mornings with her beagle, Dusty, and watch him chase rabbits. Since Holly was fond of the backyard rabbits, she was happy he never caught any. Dusty was good company, but Holly wanted children. She was thirty-three and saddened by every year that passed without them.

She kept hoping to come to terms with William being dead set against them. After all, her life was good, and he had said more than once he didn't have time for children. With all his trips to research and promote his books, he barely had time for her.

She headed back to the house to clean up after the houseguests and make sure they had everything they needed in their rooms. William had taken the guests on a wine tasting tour of Sonoma vineyards close by. The breakfast dishes were left on the table, and four more friends were coming for dinner. There was plenty of work to be done.

William had hired a caterer for the dinner. She was a visiting chef from Canada, who catered a sumptuous dinner for his book publisher. Holly was glad for any help, but she was also disappointed because she loved to cook and everybody raved about her food.

After William returned with Noelle and Jacques in the late afternoon, the three of them went to lie down and sleep off the alcohol before starting again in the evening. When the caterer arrived, Holly was startled by her appearance. Sofia was a beautiful young woman with dark hair in a stylish short cut, just like the woman William had written into his most recent story.

Sofia made a delicious dinner of roast chickens, spicy green beans, and potatoes marinated in olive oil with crusty bread to mop up all the sauces. She spoke fluent French with Noelle and Jacques. Holly decided she must be from Quebec.

Jacques was an old friend of William's from school. As the evening progressed, he moved around the table and became more flirtatious with all the women, often leaving

THREE BULLFIGHTS

Noelle on her own. When everyone had finished eating and Holly was finally relaxing at the table, he wandered over to sit by her. He said, "You must come and stay at my apartment in Paris."

She looked across the table and was sad to see Noelle watching them so closely. She said, "I'd love to come to Paris this spring. I'll ask William what his schedule's like for May."

"The apartment is available any time. Either with or without him." Jacques winked, putting his hand over hers.

Holly excused herself to go and check on things in the kitchen. When she got there, she saw William and Sofia laughing together at the kitchen sink. She left without saying a word and was embarrassed about it afterwards. She thought she was probably being overly sensitive about the flirting.

Later that evening when William came to bed, she said, "Noelle seems sad. She didn't talk much tonight." Holly put her book, *Desert Solitaire*, down on the bed beside her.

"She never does. She's been depressed for years. I don't know how he puts up with it." William said. He went in the bathroom, brushed his teeth, and bumped into the chair on his way back. Holly remembered the time he had mistaken the closet for the bathroom and peed on her shoes.

"She seems like such an interesting woman. The photographs of her artwork were amazing. I hope she's got a good therapist back in France." Holly picked the book up and started to read again.

"She tried to commit suicide last year, so the therapist can't be *that* good. She tried a few years ago too. I think she's just a nutcase." William climbed into bed beside her and quickly fell asleep.

Holly said to William's back, "She doesn't seem like a nutcase to me."

~~

They went to Paris later in the spring. Jacques met them at the apartment to hand over the keys and arranged to see them later for dinner at a restaurant down the street. William decided to take a walk around the neighborhood while Holly took a nap.

When they arrived at the restaurant, Jacques waved to them from a corner table. He introduced them to a friend of his, Simone, who was snuggled up next to him in the booth. She was a fashionable woman with a pretty smile who worked as a flight attendant for Air France. They ate garlicky escargot and shared a carafe of white wine.

Jacques and Simone seemed to know each other's habits as if they'd been together for years. They'd just returned from a trip to Nîmes and raved about the town.

Jacques said, "Nîmes is the most Roman town outside Italy. There are Roman temples, aqueducts, and an arena *fabuleuse*. You should try to get down there while you're here."

Simone asked, "Didn't we see a poster saying the annual Nîmes fair was this week? You were grouchy for the whole day afterwards because we were going to miss it." She pouted and prodded him in the stomach.

"That's right!" Jacques said, "You have to go! I'm sure the hotels are all booked, but you can stay in a nearby town. My apartment will still be empty when you get back."

William said, "In that case, we'll go tomorrow. If we can't find a hotel, we can always sleep in the car." Holly had slept in the car in an empty lot outside Park City, Utah when William had to experience the Sundance Film Festival. She didn't love it, but it was part of the package.

Back at the apartment, Holly unpacked a few things and got ready for bed. William sat at a table near the window drinking the brandy he'd bought earlier on his walk.

"Have you ever met Simone before?" she asked.

William looked up from his book, "No, but she seems nice so I'm happy for him."

"What about Noelle? I thought they were married."

"This is France. Being married doesn't mean you don't see other people."

"I'm glad we're American then." She pulled up the blankets and turned over onto her side away from William's light.

The next day they were on their way to Nîmes. After a full day of driving, William found a basic hotel in a small nearby town with only a bakery and convenience store. They had cheese and bread for dinner, but as long as Holly had a bed to sleep in, she didn't care.

The next morning, they finished the drive, parked in the outskirts of Nîmes, and walked into town. Costumed people wandered the streets, and brass bands were already assembling. Holly and William stopped at a tent café and had croissants, coffee, and beer for breakfast.

They spent the rest of the morning peering in small museums and walking down rows of arts and crafts stalls. Around lunchtime, they bought crepes and sat in the grass to watch parade horses perform in a formal garden.

Mid-afternoon, they found themselves at the Roman Amphitheater, a tremendously impressive structure. It had two tiers of soaring arcades and was as high as a ten-story building. William figured the arena inside was as big as a football field.

He went to the ticket office to look at the day's events and came back beaming, "There's a bullfight going on right now. I bought tickets. Let's go!"

Holly said, "I don't want to go to another bullfight."

"It's okay. They don't kill the bull in France. I promise. The Romans used the arena in Nîmes for gladiator fights. You'll never get to see it in action like this again."

"As long as you're sure about it," Holly said. She wanted to see the architectural details inside and followed after William.

When they walked in, the bullfight was already in progress. Since the amphitheater held over twenty thousand spectators, there were plenty of seats to choose from. Holly noticed the bull had three banderillos stabbed in each shoulder.

THREE BULLFIGHTS

She wondered how they dealt with the stab wounds if they didn't kill the bull. Did they stitch them up at the end of the fight?

The matador seemed very sure of himself and knelt in front of the bull before plunging his sword cleanly between the shoulder blades. Remembering William's promise, Holly reasoned it must be a trick sword. But when the bull fell over and the men started to saw off his ears and tail, she felt stupid and foolish.

Her first instinct was to simply get up and leave, but William had the keys to the car, and she'd never find him again in the crowd. She looked over and said, "You lied! Let's get out of here."

William looked shocked. "I thought I was right. Listen, I'm going to stay for a little while. I'll meet you at that café where we had breakfast near the car."

As she started to walk away, he said, "Aren't you glad you got to see it anyway?"

~ III ~

Mexico was Holly's favorite country. Her best friend from her New Mexico high school days was a lively girl named Marta who was originally from 'Old' Mexico. She wore colorful shawls and braided her long black hair like Frida Kahlo.

The summer after their graduation, Holly and Marta went on a monthlong trip to Mexico, traveling the country by bus and staying with people Marta knew. Holly loved it and studied Spanish throughout college with the hopes of spending more time there.

Holly and William had arrived in Mazatlán on Mexico's Pacific coast for a two-week vacation. Holly remembered the city well from her first trip and was relieved it still had an authentic part of town away from the big hotels. William liked anywhere he could go deep-sea fishing, swim, and lie in the sand. He planned to have a real vacation and not to do any work while they were there.

It was a celebration of sorts. After fourteen years, William had finally agreed to having a child, and Holly surprised herself at forty by getting pregnant the third month they tried. It was still early days, so they hadn't told anyone yet, but they both wanted to do something special.

They found a small hotel with big windows that opened onto the ocean and a full-length porch outside. The room was sparkling white with dark rattan furniture, and the interior balcony looked down on a central courtyard with a garden full of bougainvillea and palms and a restaurant jauntily named *El Shrimp Bucket.*

They swam in the ocean every morning, ate a late lunch, and had a siesta. They liked *El Shrimp Bucket*'s spicy food for breakfast and had fresh ceviche for lunch at an outdoor restaurant down the street.

One day at lunch, they saw a table of six young Mexican men and women drinking *cervezas* and doling out pesos to a

THREE BULLFIGHTS

Mariachi band. They gave the band a list of songs and knew all the words to every verse, singing boisterously along.

Before long, Holly and William were invited and moved over to the table. By the end of the afternoon, they were dancing with the young people on the sidewalk. When the Mariachis eventually needed to leave, everyone tipped them well and settled their tabs with the waiter.

William said, "That was an amazing afternoon. I've had so much tequila I can hardly walk." He thanked everyone and said, "We should meet here at the same time tomorrow!"

One of the women at the table was named Paulina. She was a striking girl in her twenties with tightly pulled back hair, pale blue eyes, and impeccable English. She said, "I would like to take you to my father's farm instead. It's *muy bonita* and peaceful and not so far away."

"We'd love to go," William said. He and Holly got up from the table, and everyone kissed cheeks to say goodbye.

He stumbled on the uneven pavement as they walked away so Holly slipped her arm through his. She said, "Don't worry, I'll get you back. I wasn't drinking."

After breakfast the next morning, Paulina and two of the young men picked them up at the hotel. Paulina pointed out the important landmarks of the town while the men, who looked hungover, remained silent. All three of them made the sign of the cross every time they saw a church.

About two miles from their destination, Paulina said, "My father's land starts here."

Fields stretched out on either side. Many had rows of workers bent over picking produce with their heads covered by swaths of cloth.

They arrived at a newly built hacienda and were served shrimp netted by the staff earlier that same morning. Paulina showed them every room of the house, including her parent's bedroom. She seemed to be at a loss for what to do next, so they all went outside and stared across the landscape.

The young men started up two gas scooters from a nearby shed and offered to take Holly and William on a tour of the farm. They squeezed in behind the drivers and rode down the dirt roads between the fields. They drove past men, women, and children working silently in long-sleeved rags, meager protection from the sun. When the people looked up to watch the noisy bikes pass, Holly nodded but was too ashamed to wave.

Back at the house, Holly went to the bathroom and discovered she was bleeding. She and William took Paulina aside to ask about a doctor and what she thought they should do.

Paulina said, "My aunt is a nurse who works at the local hospital. I'll call her and have her meet us there."

The trip back to Mazatlán seemed slow, and Holly's cramps got worse by the minute. She kept shifting her position and hoped she wouldn't stain the car before they got there.

THREE BULLFIGHTS

Paulina's aunt, Gabriela, met them at the entrance. She put her arm around Holly and took her inside to change and see the doctor. William stayed behind to wait in the courtyard.

The doctor found that Holly was in the middle of a miscarriage, did an operation to complete it, and recommended she stay in the hospital overnight. William sat with her for a while then went to find a cab for himself before it got dark. He promised to be back early the next morning.

When Paulina's aunt Gabriela came to visit at the end of her shift, Holly was comforted by her kind eyes and the old-fashioned nursing cap. She spoke simple Spanish that was easy to understand. Holly had been brave when William was there, but when Gabriela sat down beside her, the tears flowed.

She asked, "Why did this happen to our baby? What did I do wrong?"

Gabriela held her hand and said, "You did nothing wrong. A miscarriage is nature's way of ending a pregnancy that's not normal. It happens more often than you think."

"But why would I have an abnormal pregnancy?" Holly used the sheet to wipe her eyes and checked her hospital gown for blood.

"It happens more with older mothers, but lots of them get pregnant again and have healthy babies. You can try again in a couple of months." Gabriela brought a cup of water to Holly and encouraged her to drink.

"I'm not sure my husband will want to try again," Holly said glumly.

Gabriela sat with her for an hour and actually made her laugh with tales of growing up in Mexico. She gave Holly her phone number before she left and said, "*Llámame cuando lo necesites.* Call me anytime. I mean it."

When William came the next morning, Holly said, "I know we're supposed to spend another week here, but I want to go home. I feel too sad to be on a vacation."

~~

Back in California, Holly was exhausted and stayed in bed several days to recover. William wandered aimlessly around the house then abruptly announced he was going to Colorado for a few days to do research for a new book.

By the time William returned, she felt a little better, but the sadness still came in waves. In her excitement about the pregnancy, she'd allowed herself to dream of a different life ahead with a baby. Now all her plans were ruined.

It was hard to get William to talk about how he felt about the loss. One sunny morning when they were walking Dusty on the hills behind the house, Holly decided to give it another try.

"Are you still sad about losing the baby? You're stoic, but I know it must hurt you too."

"It does, but I wasn't as committed to the idea. Maybe it wasn't meant to be," William said. He threw a stick down the hill and Dusty retrieved it.

THREE BULLFIGHTS

"Losing a pregnancy early on happens all the time. After another month, we'll be able to try again." Holly smiled to look encouraging.

"I'm not sure I want to try again. I hate to say it, but more scheduled sex would be a drag not a pleasure." William picked up his pace.

Holly stopped walking. "Other couples manage to go through months of this without complaining. Why are you being so insensitive and uncooperative?"

"I guess I was never excited about having children to begin with." William turned down the hill to walk back to the house.

Holly called to Dusty and continued down the path. William's response was more or less what she'd expected, and she knew it was pointless to press him any further. In William's world, women were either convenient or inconvenient, and she was becoming increasingly inconvenient.

William left for another trip the next week. He said he was writing a book about cowboys that involved research in the Old West. Holly pretended to be asleep the morning he left so that she wouldn't have to hug him goodbye. Midmorning, she went to the kitchen to feed Dusty and brought a cup of tea and cookies back to bed.

After giving it some thought, she decided to make herself useful and straighten up the bedroom. She picked up the pile of coins from the Mexican trip on William's dresser to put them downstairs with the foreign money. When she looked at them more closely, she was puzzled to find a few Canadian coins mixed in with the Mexican ones. William had never taken a trip to Canada that she knew about, and they had no Canadian friends. The only Canadian person she could think of was Sofia the caterer.

She went to William's office and opened the drawer where all the foreign money was kept. She saw more Canadian coins there as well as some Canadian bills. Trembling, she returned the coins in her hand to William's dresser upstairs exactly as she'd found them.

She thought about confronting William with her suspicions but decided that would only lead to more strife. Despite his flaws, she loved William and couldn't imagine her life without him. He was much more important than the prospect of a child, and her reproductive years were almost finished.

When William returned from his trip, Holly managed to suppress her feelings and say nothing. The next month, he invited her to join him on another trip to Mexico, this time with his English friend Eric. She liked Eric. He was a soft-spoken man with a good sense of humor.

They went to Zacatecas in the heart of Mexico's cowboy country. Holly had never traveled there before and enjoyed the old architecture and the lively town squares. It had an active silver mine, an impressive central cathedral, and an open-air market with silver-studded saddles and bridles. She carried a pad with her and did many drawings of the town.

THREE BULLFIGHTS

Zacatecas formerly had a bullring, but it had been turned into a hotel. They went there for drinks one night, and William walked downstairs to the middle of the arena, where he turned and took a bow. When Eric said he'd always wanted to see a bullfight, Holly wanted to shout, "Are you crazy?" but said nothing. She was afraid even a small outburst might risk breaking the dam inside her.

They ate burritos with beef jerky every morning for breakfast outside their hotel and watched the cowboys ride their horses into town. In the late afternoon, they sipped mezcal at a table facing the sunset.

Near the end of the trip, Eric found a poster advertising a bullfight to be held the next day, the day of their departure. They were scheduled for an evening flight from Guadalajara, a four-hour drive from Zacatecas, and the bullring was along the Zacatecas-Guadalajara road. William and Eric calculated there was just enough time to go to the bullfight and then drive straight to the airport to make the flight.

They told Holly about the plan over mezcals that afternoon. Back in their room getting ready for dinner, Holly told William she didn't want to go to another bullfight. He said there would be too little time to return to Zacatecas to pick her up from the hotel and suggested she read her book in the car during the bullfight instead.

The next day, they drove out in the late morning and after an hour's drive turned off into a parking lot with an undistinguished bullring squatting next to it. There were only about fifty parked cars, and the uneven gravel glinted with broken glass. Eric had bought three tickets the day before. William handed her one before he and Eric headed over to the bullring.

The car was hot, so Holly rolled down the windows. It wasn't long before a boy around eight years old appeared at the window with Chiclets gum. His hair was cut very short, and his face was as dirty as his torn T-shirt. She decided to buy a packet in the hopes he would go away.

She noticed in her wallet that she still had the slip of paper with the phone number of Gabriela the nurse. She gave the child all her small coins, but he kept hanging around, so she rolled up the windows. He stayed outside pressing his face to the glass and yelling to some rough looking teenagers across the parking lot.

She rapidly exited the other side, locked the car, and walked quickly into the bullring. It was easy to find William and Eric because they were the only pale faces inside.

She glanced into the arena and saw it was a small black cow, not a bull, that the matador was fighting. The cow tried to run away and was chased back to the middle by two men who beat her flanks with sticks. When the matador struck her with his sword, she fell on her side moaning in pain. They tried to get her to stand up, but she refused. The matador knelt down to kill her, and her blood spread out quickly to cover the ground beneath her.

Eric put his arm around Holly, who was sobbing uncontrollably, to lead her back to the car. She looked back and saw William spit into the bullring in disgust before he

THREE BULLFIGHTS

followed behind them. She supposed he had not enjoyed the show.

Back at the car, Holly unlocked the door, removed her backpack and suitcase from the backseat, and handed the keys to Eric. A line of taxis waited at the edge of the parking lot.

"What are you doing?" William asked.

"I'm not going to Guadalajara. I've decided to take a bus to Mazatlán."

"You're not thinking clearly. You need to calm down. I can't let you go on your own," William said.

"I am calm, and I am going on my own," Holly said goodbye to Eric and walked over to one of the taxis.

"I'm worried about you. Where will you be?" William followed her.

"I'm sure there'll be rooms available at the hotel over *El Shrimp Bucket*," Holly said. She told the driver to take her to the bus station.

William looked in the taxi window and took her hand. "Please call me when you get there, Holly."

When she arrived, she called Gabriela instead.

TOUGH ENOUGH

The Dean's white coat shone from the podium. His top pocket was monogrammed with red initials and a stethoscope peeked out from his lower one. The auditorium was ostentatious and large. Alice and her new classmates occupied only the first four rows and his words echoed in the empty space behind them.

"You are the chosen ones. There were plenty of applicants for each slot. Ten other capable students wanted to sit just where you're sitting right now. But you won the honor to be in this place for this welcoming ceremony because you were the best. We chose you because you were the smartest in your class and the most accomplished. We knew you were the ones who had the potential to achieve great things.

The bottom line is this: We know you're smart enough. The big question now remaining is: Are you tough enough? We lose about twenty percent of our medical students during the first year. Look around you. You'll be missing quite a few people sitting in your row by the end of the year. Who will it be? Will you be the one who disappoints all the people who helped you get here? Will you disappoint yourself?"

Alice looked down her row. The most obvious thing was that there weren't many other women. All this chest thumping made her squirm because she knew the macho culture that came with it. She figured the other women did too. What had she signed up for, the Marines?

She'd been encouraged to pursue medicine at the insistence of her biology instructor, but it had not been a lifelong ambition. She didn't want to assume she was the best and brightest in any crowd, and she probably wasn't cut out to achieve great things.

The Dean announced, "Tomorrow in anatomy class you'll start dissecting cadavers."

On her walk home, Alice wondered, what did tough enough even mean? Tough enough to study hard and beat everyone else? Tough enough to withstand the blood and gore? Tough enough to absorb an unwarranted amount of abuse?

Her dog, Sam, was exuberant when she walked in the door. So much better than the rabbit named Buns, she'd inherited from a friend a few years earlier, who was totally still and expressionless when she picked him up. Alice sat on the floor, and Sam climbed onto her lap. He gave her a loving look and a lick on the face.

She'd rescued Sam from the shelter when he was six months old. It was hard to imagine someone giving up a big, cuddly black Labrador, but their loss was her gain. Now Sam was almost two, and she couldn't imagine life without him.

The career she'd really wished for as a child was to become a veterinarian. She decided against it as an adult because she felt too emotional about animals suffering. When her biology teacher talked to her about medicine, she thought she might be less emotional about people. But she sometimes wondered about her decision to study medicine since she didn't even like people very much.

It wasn't that her life had been difficult or that her parents had been monsters. She'd grown up as an only child in a middle-class neighborhood with parents who were so deeply in love and involved with each other, that there seemed to be no room for anything else. Their indifference led to hers. She learned to play by herself, which meant with the dogs.

Since her mother and father had been careless with the dogs, there'd been quite a few. There was a beagle called Tigger, a poodle named Georgie, a sheepdog called Jigs, two little Welsh Terriers named Prince and Katie, and an Airedale named Duke. Alice saved their collars and carried them with her from place to place.

Almost all of the dogs met their end under the wheels of a car. When she was young, Alice had a hard time remembering the various places where the dogs were buried. She made vain attempts to mark the graves herself, but even her more creative markers disappeared within a week or two, and she suspected her parents were the culprits. Once, to her horror, another animal had even tried to dig up one of her dogs after only a few days.

~~

It had been challenging to find the perfect apartment with Sam in tow. The one she chose was close enough to school so Alice could come home for lunch. Since Sam was going to be trapped at home all day, she decided against the dark apartment with a big bathroom and looked for one with more windows instead. She liked an old fireplace in another one, but she knew Sam would like outside space even better.

This apartment had a small patch of backyard surrounded by a tall peeling fence. There was a deep sofa for Sam to lie on in the front room next to the window and industrial metal bowls for food and water on the linoleum tiles in the kitchen. And the bedroom was big enough for a king bed, which she needed, because Sam turned in giant circles before he sprawled out across half the bed.

Alice and Sam had spent the summer going to the beach and taking long walks to explore the town, and now they knew their way around. She picked up his leash from a bowl by the door, and they headed out to the nearby park.

The South Carolina sky was dense with clouds, and the air was heavy and hot. Going outside in September still felt like a warm, wet washcloth had hit you in the face. Sam was panting but his eyes weren't bulging out as much as they had been in June.

The wide Charleston porches were deserted because everyone was indoors with their air conditioners on full blast. Alice thought the ornate porches must have been much more useful in the old days. Now they were just an extra place to sweep. She felt an unusual pang of homesickness for New York. The trees in the Hudson Valley would be just starting to change color around now and the mornings would have a slight chill in the air.

Sam liked this walk, but it was not Alice's favorite. It led down to a shallow cement pond named Colonial Lake, which had a few shaggy Palmetto trees on the corners. There were stately old houses on the streets that ran either side, but very few people ever walked around it. Sam liked to peer into the water and had jumped in more than once chasing fish.

When they got home, Sam walked over to his bowl and she poured out some dinner. Alice was a vegetarian so she bought vegetarian dog food. She was happy Sam's health didn't seem to suffer from not eating meat. She'd once bought him dog food with salmon as a treat, but he didn't eat it with any more gusto than his usual brand.

After dinner, Alice began to worry about her classes and her schedule. The thought of leaving Sam alone for many hours tomorrow, the rest of the week, and every week to follow made her feel sad. She decided to run a few miles with him in the mornings to exhaust him enough so he'd want to lie around all day.

She felt apprehensive about her classmates because she was still awkward and shy around people. She hoped her social reluctance wouldn't stand out as much in medical school as it had in high school and college, since everyone would need to study.

She also couldn't help thinking about the cadavers. She wondered what they looked like and how a room full dead bodies would feel.

The next morning it felt a little cooler on the way to anatomy class. Alice braced herself for the crowd when she walked in the room and found her assigned table easily. Two classmates already stood by the body, which was draped with a sheet. She shyly introduced herself to them. Bob was quite a bit older, looked conventionally Southern, and wore a tie under his white coat. Matt was more her age, had longer hair, and was wearing jeans with what looked like a Rolling Stones T-shirt under his.

After Bob removed the sheet, Alice glanced at the cadaver's face then quickly moved to stand by the feet. She found herself right above the toe tag. It was tightly attached by a wire that almost cut through the yellowed skin of the big toe. The name was handwritten on beige paper with a quant flourish. Mr. Ramey had died from a gunshot wound that had torn right through his heart and was younger than most of the other cadavers in the room. Alice thought that at least, he'd died quickly.

An hour later, Alice, Bob, and Matt went to the auditorium where their lectures were held. It was a windowless, well-worn room in the middle of a block of university buildings on one of Charleston's busiest streets. It had seating for two hundred and a sizable stage.

She put her books in the seat beside Matt, but since she didn't know him very well, she went over to peruse the brass plaques on the wall commemorating the doctors who had come before. Dr Newman was 'An Example to All' and Dr Cathcart was "A Distinguished Researcher." Dr Phillips was "A Hero in Medicine," whatever that meant.

The classes felt like a relief after the cadavers, and she was just getting sleepy around eleven o'clock when the sound of many dogs barking almost drowned out the lecturer. She looked over at Matt with alarm. The noise quieted down a little and was replaced with sporadic howls, which continued until the end of the class.

"What was that?" Alice asked as soon as the lecturer had left the stage.

"There must be a dog lab next door," Bob said.

"It doesn't sound like a very nice place," Alice said. She stood up, eager to get home to Sam for lunch.

'Don't worry, I'll ask my uncle tonight. He trained here as a surgeon not so long ago and probably sat in this same classroom," Matt said, "Maybe it was a one-time thing."

She had tears in her eyes when Sam climbed in her lap after she got home. She gave him a big hug and stood up. When she walked towards the bowl with the leash, he went crazy. They had a quick stroll and ate peanut butter sandwiches for lunch.

In anatomy class the next day, Bob, Matt, and Alice started the dissection of Mr. Ramey's shoulder. They worked above his chest where the gunshot had entered. His pectoral muscle was thick and had burnt around the tattered edges. It looked like charred steak.

Matt said, "I spoke to my uncle and I'm afraid there is an animal lab next door. The staff comes in at eleven. That must be what all the dogs are barking about. They feed them and do the lab work after that."

Alice said, "You mean the howling part."

"Yep."

Bob said, "I heard lab dogs are excited to see you no matter what you do to them. They say the monkeys are the worst. They hate you after the first day because they know what's coming."

Later that morning, Alice checked her watch three times in the auditorium so she could brace herself for eleven o'clock. When the dogs started barking, it still broke her heart. She wondered if she'd be able to stand it for another four years. Maybe she wasn't tough enough after all.

She was ashamed of all the times she'd put her feelings aside when she was studying biology in college. She spent her childhood picking up frogs to pat their little heads and collecting turtles to feed them lettuce. Her mother had even given her two white rats to take care of, who slept in a cage at the foot of her bed.

After only a few semesters of biology lab, she'd betrayed all those creatures she loved so much. She cut the heads off frogs to watch them swim without a brain. She cut the hearts out of big, beautiful turtles to see how long they beat outside the body. And she guillotined the lab rats who had been friendly to her even after she'd injected them daily with strange chemicals.

She toyed with the idea of skipping the eleven o'clock class, but she learned much more from the lectures than the notetaking service's endless pages. Her only option was to get used to the barking. It was going to be harder to get used to the howling dogs than getting used to Mr. Ramey.

That weekend she took Sam to the beach early on Sunday morning. Dogs could be off leash in the mornings, and she loved to watch him running in the waves and swimming in the ocean. When he ran back from the water to catch up with her, she was sure she could see him smiling.

Many of the dogs in the lab had deep barks that sounded like they were bigger dogs. She wished she could take them all in her car and let them out on the beach to run. She wondered how small their cages were.

~~

That winter was cold and rainy, but Alice still managed to run almost every morning with Sam. He was oblivious to the rain and the cold, and Alice had sensible New York coats to keep her warm and dry. It was often impossible to run in the Hudson Valley because of the deep snow.

One morning in the early spring, Alice, Bob, and Matt found maggots in Mr. Ramey's wound. It was hard to know how long they had been there, since for the last two months they'd been dissecting the arms and the legs. Bob learned from one of the anatomy professors that a lighter formalin solution had been used, and there were maggots in other bodies as well. The professor's plan was to cut off body parts, either when the dissection was finished or when maggots were discovered; whichever came first.

Alice had never seen maggots before, and she certainly hadn't expected to see hundreds of them squirming in a human body. She was quieter than usual as she helped cut away the maggot-ridden muscle. Matt and Bob asked if she wanted to come with them for a beer at McCrady's Pub after class, but she said she needed to go home and feed the dog.

When she got home, she took Sam on their usual walk, and then he sprawled out across the sofa with his head on her knee.

"Oh Sam, medical school is getting more and more disgusting. Even you would be appalled. It was bad enough to have to hack through that soupy pink tissue and pretend to see the things you were supposed to see. Now, it's crawling with maggots."

Sam looked up at her sympathetically.

"One of our instructors wants to *be* a cadaver when he dies. He says he'll be the perfect specimen. How weird is that?" she asked. Sam knew it was a question because of the inflection in her voice, but he had no answer.

"I'm feeling even less convinced I'm cut out for this. I should've gone to veterinary school so I could take care of animals like you." Sam sighed happily when she gave him a scratch on the ears. Resting her cheek against his soft fur, Alice thought hard about her alternatives and shed a few tears. She didn't want to be part of the twenty percent of students who drop out in the first year.

She sat back up, "From the time I was your age, I wanted to prove to everybody that women are just as tough as men. I guess this is my chance."

Sam sat up too and licked her nose, which usually meant he agreed.

~~

In the end, Mr. Ramey had so little maggot-free flesh left that they had to change to another cadaver. Mrs. Baker weighed two hundred and fifty pounds and posed her own special challenges. In the meantime, Alice had decided that she wanted to become a surgeon. She knew that talking to patients in an office all day would be a challenge for her. And there weren't many women surgeons.

There had not been a single day of class without hearing the dogs barking from the lab next door. And every day, Alice thought about how miserable their lives were. It was sad to think that, even though humans caused them pain, they still barked and wagged their tails when they saw them come in the lab in the mornings.

In the late spring, after the eleven o'clock lecture, Bob told Alice, "The anatomy professor says we're going to be operating on dogs next week."

She was stunned. "Why would we do that?"

"He says it really helps understand how things work in a living body. It's the logical next step now that we're almost finished with the cadavers."

Bob had been a pharmacist before and liked to chat with many of the professors. Bob, Alice, and Matt were often the first students to know what was coming next.

"Oh God. The last thing I want to do is operate on dogs," Alice said.

"I can ask my uncle if they made them do it." Matt said.

"Thanks Matt, but I bet they did. This is probably some time-honored rite of passage." Alice said.

She asked Bob, "Did he say what kind of operations we'd be doing or how many dogs there'd be?"

"I don't know anything about the operations, but he did say there wouldn't be more than six people to a dog so everyone could do some surgery and see what was going on."

Alice figured that since there were one hundred and sixty students, it would mean twenty to thirty dogs. She stood up and clutched her books to her chest.

"I may be sick all next week," she said to Bob and Matt.

Bob said, "I think we're going to have two dog labs, so it may be hard to avoid. And you said you wanted to be a surgeon so now you can see what it's really like."

Later that afternoon, Alice sat with Sam in the back yard. He had found a sliver of light and was stretched out on his side in the dirt with the sun falling on his face. She was drinking a beer and eating potato chips. She occasionally threw one his way.

She couldn't stop her mind from racing and every thought was about how awful it would be to operate on a dog. Sam started whimpering. She looked down and realized he was dreaming. All four feet were jerking back and forth so she figured he must be chasing something.

She hardly slept the night before the dog lab, so she wasn't able to run with Sam the next morning. He jumped up to stand by the door every time she passed the bowl with the leash. She gave him breakfast and promised him a big walk at the end of the day.

~~

Her class met in the anatomy lab and was taken upstairs after a vague, and barely adequate, briefing. They were told their operating tables would be in alphabetical order, just as their cadavers were in anatomy lab, but with two groups per dog. Alice made a wish that all the dog surgeries would be minimal procedures that wouldn't cause much pain and would heal quickly.

Her resolve faltered when she walked into the room. There were twenty-five tables with big, beautiful dogs stretched out on them sleeping. She'd never seen so many dogs in one room before.

She couldn't look anywhere but at the floor without crying. She followed close behind Matt who found their table.

TOUGH ENOUGH

Their dog was a female, a black Labrador mix about the same size as Sam. She somehow had expected something smaller.

One of the lab assistants set down the instruments and gave Bob the razor to shave the abdomen and the soap to prep the area. While he was doing that, Alice, Matt, and the other three students scrubbed, gowned, and gloved. Alice was feeling more panic stricken as time went on. She tried her hardest to pretend to be calm. When Bob had scrubbed himself, he turned to Alice and said, "Since you're the best with a knife, you should make the incision. The tech said it's supposed to be midline and vertical in the lower abdomen."

Alice stood over the dog and was overwhelmed by how much the skin and wet fur smelled like Sam. She also now realized the surgeries they were performing were not going to be minor, but still hoped their team might do something useful like spaying the dog. The smell of the wet fur and the lifelessness of the dog made her feel like she was going to faint.

She gave the scalpel back to Bob and said, "No, you can do it. I have to sit down,"

Bob said, "I'm surprised. You're usually so tough. You didn't even flinch when Mr. Ramey's bile got all over your shoes."

"I'm sure I'll be fine in a minute." She sat on a stool some distance from where they were working and tried to keep her gown and gloves as sterile as possible. She was glad the mask obscured her tears, but she wondered about her gown staying sterile since they were dripping off her chin.

She watched the lab assistants come by several times. All the voices were muffled by the masks so she couldn't understand what anyone was saying. Bob's gloves were bloody so she knew they must be doing something, but she still felt too weak and nauseated to get up.

After about fifteen minutes, she gathered her strength and walked over to the table. She purposefully stood behind Matt so she couldn't see the incision. She asked him, "Did you spay her?"

"No, they just wanted us to see everything: stomach, intestines, liver and aorta. He had a worried look in his eyes, "The tech is coming back in a few minutes. You might want to go back and sit down."

"Why?" asked Alice.

"Because now we're going to cut the ribs and observe the heart and lungs."

"How will she ever recover from that?" Alice gasped.

Matt hesitated a minute, then said, "She won't. They put them down afterwards. In fact, they want us to cut out the heart so we can see the large vessels coming in and out of it."

Bob looked up from across the table and said, "The tech told me that they all have heartworms and are going to die anyway."

Alice asked, "How do they know that?" She could hear the tell-tale sob in her voice. She felt like a ten-year-old pleading against the inevitable.

"I think almost all strays have them in this state. Listen Alice, I know this is upsetting but you've got to remember these are dogs not people."

Alice realized she would have preferred it the other way around.

She said, "I want the heart."

Matt asked, "You mean you want to look at it after we take it out?"

"No, I mean I want it. I want to take it home. I'm going to scrub out and get a plastic bag."

Matt said, "That's pretty weird, but I guess it's okay."

Alice said, "They'll never know and I'm sure they won't care. I know it doesn't make much sense but having it will make me feel better."

Matt promised to keep it for her. He said he thought it should be out in about twenty minutes and they'd put it in a metal basin to one side. Bob and the other students looked at her like she was crazy.

She stumbled back over to her stool and wiped her face with her gloved hands. She resisted her urge to scream as she looked out across the room filled with students covered in dog blood and dogs who were dying on the tables. She took off her gown and gloves and threw them in the trash.

It was a long trudge back home carrying the bag with the heart. Sam was curious about the plastic bag as soon as she walked in the door, but she thought it was probably because the smell of blood was new to him. She put it in her refrigerator then attached the leash to take him on the long walk she'd promised.

It was a beautiful day and the city was bursting with flowers, but that made it hurt even worse. She felt complicit in the slaughter. She kept going over all the things she ought to have done. She knew they would have been futile, but at least she might have felt better about herself than she did right now. They walked all the way to the old marina, and she sat on a beat-up bench looking out over the water. Sam was totally quiet. He was usually subdued when there were no smiles, and she was silent.

She decided to name the lab dog Tessa since she may not have had a real name, or if she did, it was long forgotten. The idea of creating some sort of a memorial for her was the only thing that gave Alice any solace.

When she and Sam returned home, she called her landlord to see if she could bury a small part of an animal in the back yard behind her apartment. He was sympathetic and agreeable. She then found a company in the Yellow Pages that made gravestones and ordered a bronze memorial marker.

She'd only put a stick in the ground for Tigger, but she remembered making a rag doll for Georgie and a sock monkey for Jigs. She'd glued Prince and Katie's initials in sequins on the bottom of their bowls and sunk them in the ground. And she found a beautiful round river stone for Duke.

She decided to ask her parents if they remembered all her grave markers, the next time she talked to them. They'd both become even more isolated and dependent on each other with age. She dreaded the day when one of them died.

Returning to class the next day was difficult, but Matt and Bob didn't ask many questions. Bob was considerate enough to let her know when the next dog lab was scheduled so she could call in sick that day. She was relieved that gross anatomy was almost finished. It was aptly named, and she'd had more than enough of it at this point.

She bought a shovel over the weekend and dug a deep hole in the corner of the yard near the back fence. She kept Sam in the apartment while she took the heart out of the plastic bag and buried it. When she let him out, he went over to sniff the upturned dirt, but didn't show much interest.

In her last week of classes, she resolved to continue with medical school the next year, despite all her misgivings. And she still wanted to be a surgeon, despite her failure with the dogs. Operating on people to help them would be much easier than killing helpless animals.

She signed a lease to stay in the apartment and planned to keep it for the next three years. Sam was used to the routine, and she didn't want to change anything for either of their sakes.

The gravestone company called her to say the bronze plaque was ready. It was surprisingly heavy when she carried it out to the car. She stopped by a florist on the way home and picked out some lilies that she placed by the fence in a pink plastic cup.

She got the shovel, then carried the heavy plaque from the car to the corner of the back yard. The dirt was hard and dry, and she was covered in sweat by the time the hole was deep enough to place the plaque securely.

She sat on the ground by the grave and wiped it clean with a cloth. Sam climbed into her lap and they admired it together, although only she could read it.

It said: To Tessa who gave us the gift of a dog's heart.

A WINTER IN SOMERSET

"How's it look?" Sarah asked Tom. She put her phone on speaker, ate another spoonful of Grape Nuts, and watched the sparrows gather for the breadcrumbs she'd scattered on the 10th floor windowsill of her tiny apartment on First Avenue.

"It's big. We'll both have a bedroom to use for office space and still have one leftover for guests. It has two fireplaces downstairs and lots of windows. I'm at the kitchen window now and there are cows outside." Tom noticed the cows were knee deep in mud, but they looked healthy.

"English cows?" Sarah asked.

"They're not drinking tea, if that's what you mean. They're English Jersey cows but I don't think it's a working dairy farm. There's an amazing looking pub across the street."

"Perfect! Tell them we'll take it. I'm headed over to the hospital now. Call me tomorrow when you're back in London and on the way home."

The pieces of Sarah and Tom's year in England were finally falling into place. It was the most adventurous thing either of them had ever embarked upon, and, most importantly, the first time they were going to actually live together in the same place. They'd both grown up on farms and were excited to find the house because they were curious about how everything worked on a British farm.

TOUGH ENOUGH: TEN STORIES

Sarah was finishing up an obstetrics residency in New York City and was known as 'the hippie' among her fellow residents. She had unruly blonde curls and a full set of acupuncture needles from her previous career as an acupuncturist. Tom was tall and quiet and polite. He still said 'yes ma'am' or 'no sir' when answering questions from anyone past adolescence.

They'd met at a barbeque for hospital workers on the Navajo reservation in Tuba City. The one sheep who attended the party was extremely popular with the children until she got her throat cut. Following that, the doctors gathered up their wailing families and dispersed within minutes. They weren't aware that killing sheep was so central to the Navajo culture that all the Miss Navajo pageant contestants had to excel at it.

Sarah and Tom had been happy to find they were the only two people remaining at the barbeque who weren't Navajo. They struck up a long conversation, made jokes with the Navajo about American squeamishness, when it came to killing animals, and stayed until the party was over. Neither of them had eaten a four-year-old ewe before, and neither of them planned to do it again afterwards.

In the years that followed, Tom developed a keen interest in cooking and bringing fresh food directly from farms to restaurants. After finishing his culinary training in Charleston, he found a year-long position as a chef in training at a highly renowned restaurant in Somerset, England.

Sarah had felt increasingly disillusioned about medicine in the United States during her residency training in New York

City. She thought a public health system might be the solution, so she took the British exam and found a one-year position as a doctor at the Somerset hospital.

They moved to England in September. When they drove into the muddy farmyard surrounding the large white house they'd rented, the whole Hamby family came out to greet them. The parents, Nicola and John, both looked like the farmers they had known growing up, Nicola wore an oversized Irish sweater, and John's dark green hooded coat was stained along the bottom. The whole family had on black rubber boots.

Nicola said, "Welcome! It's so good to finally meet Sarah." She had a hearty handshake. Sarah noticed the callouses from farming that covered her hand and fingers.

John put his arms around their children; Audrey, an intense dark-haired girl of fourteen and Sam, a ten-year-old who grinned at them from under his tweed cap.

John said, "Here are the two who actually run the farm. Audrey knows all about the ducks and the chickens. And if you find a lost sheep on your doorstep, come find Sam. That's his department."

Nicola said, "We were just walking over to the pub for lunch. Want to come along?"

Sarah and Tom jumped at the chance. When they walked into the low-ceilinged rooms of the pub, Sarah felt like an extra in a movie set. Most of the people inside were in their stocking feet, having left a big pile of rubber boots at the door. The front rooms had cozy fireplaces and big round tables full of families. There were glass cases with stuffed magpies and pheasants mounted on the walls.

They sat at the table and ordered pints of Bass Ale. The server, a friend of the Hambys called Joanna, placed a big bowl of roasted new potatoes in the center of the table. When John said the potatoes were from the farm down the street, Tom's eyes glowed. Sarah, who had heard bad things about English food, was hesitant about ordering the lamb with mint sauce, then discovered it was the best thing she'd ever tasted.

During lunch, Nicola entertained them with stories of when she'd lived in Italy as a student, while John quietly nodded his head and the children giggled. When they got back to the house, Sarah and Tom unpacked the few things they needed for the next day then collapsed.

After her half hour commute the next morning, Sarah was relieved to make it to the hospital in one piece. It was her first time driving on the other side of the road, and most British drivers tailgated and used the middle of the road as a passing lane, which forced her onto the shoulder for much of the trip. She sat in the Mini for a few minutes to recover. Her interview with Mr. Adam had been over a year ago, and the one-story red brick building had so many wings that it took her a minute to remember where the entrance was.

Her first hour at the hospital was spent with the nursing staff learning about proper titles. A 'Sister' in a hospital was the head nurse of a ward, and not a nun--unless she was dressed in a habit. A lively discussion ensued about what Sarah should be called, since in England surgeons were addressed as 'Mister' not 'Doctor'. They decided to call her 'Miss'.

Mr. Adam was waiting for her in the Theater, a Quonset hut behind the main building, where he planned to watch Sarah perform a caesarean delivery. She was shown the way to the nurses' changing room and was amazed to find no scrubs, only blue surgical dresses that were lowcut on top and short below, barely covering her knees. The addition of white rubber boots made for an interesting outfit when she clomped into the room.

Sarah's operation took a little more time than her usual C-sections in America, but Mr. Adam was pleased with her work. It was surprising that most of the instruments had different names in England. When she wanted a "smooth pick-up" forceps, Mr. Adam laughed and asked if it was an American drink.

After a long day and another harrowing drive, she really needed a smooth pick-up by the time she got home, and Tom had one ready for her. His first day in the restaurant had been just as confusing. Sarah noticed the house seemed cold even though there was a roaring fire in the fireplace. They huddled close to the hearth in two armchairs.

Sipping his bourbon, Tom said, "I spent most of the day mincing vegetables and learning to make Yorkshire pudding. Even at its best, it's tasteless, and the recipe is from the eighteenth century. What I can't figure out is why people are still eating it."

Sarah said, "Remind me not to order it. The highlight of my day was watching an Irish midwife do a routine delivery. It was the most beautiful thing I've ever seen."

"What was different about it?" Tom asked.

Sarah looked thoughtful and ran her hand through her curls, "I think it's because there was no sense of anything happening that wasn't exactly as it should be. It's no wonder they have such a low C-section rate here. They don't worry unless there's something to worry about." She smiled, "They brought the patient a tea tray with biscuits afterwards. It was so English!"

Tom stood up and said, "Speaking of which, what would you like for dinner? At our cozy inn here, we are proud to serve a lovely jacket potato with cheddar cheese on top or the more traditional beans on toast."

"I'll have the beans on toast, but let's make sure we get to the grocery store tomorrow to get real food."

Tom bowed and said, "Madame, we're in England. This is real food."

As the season progressed, the days got shorter and shorter, and the house got colder and colder. Sarah was on-call in the hospital two nights a week and one weekend every month. Tom's schedule was also busy, but he tried to arrange to be home the nights and days that Sarah wasn't working. They both enjoyed the weekends they spent together on the farm. They took long walks, ate at their pub, The Badger's Den, and watched the animals in the barnyard.

John Hamby was usually on machines doing heavy work, so Nicola was their source of information about the farm. The cows had been rescued from a dairy and were no longer used for milking. They'd bred them in the past, but since John kept all the calves and didn't slaughter any, it only led to more mouths to feed.

The same was true of breeding the sheep. Other English farms had ewes marked with color on their rears from the paint harnesses attached to the front of the rams, but the Hamby farm had no rams, and their sheep were snowy white. Nicola said she'd always felt sad for the lambs when they were sold for butchering, so the best solution was not to have any.

The poultry were a motley collection of different breeds of ducks and chickens, none of which were ever eaten. Audrey, their daughter, sold a few dozen chicken eggs on the weekends.

One rainy Sunday morning, Sarah put down her newspaper and said to Tom, "I know what we can do today. I've been wanting for months to go to your restaurant to see what it's like, and we've saved a little money. Let's go to lunch there today."

Tom put a couple of logs on the fire, wrapped himself back up in his blanket, and said, "The pub across the street is so much better. The endless courses we serve at the restaurant would bore you to tears. The food is decent, but it's too fussed over. And the dining room conversation is so subdued that all you hear is clinking silverware."

She put her feet on the coffee table, "I guess you're right. I would rather relax."

Tom said, "It's so expensive around here I'm impressed we've saved anything at all. How do you think the Hambys survive? As far as I can see, the money Audrey gets for eggs is all that's coming in from the farm. They're not breeding cows or sheep, and the only crop they grow is hay to feed animals that they have no plans to butcher or sell."

Sarah looked out the kitchen window. "I honestly don't know. My family made good money on alfalfa hay and sheep in New Mexico, but the grass John's baling isn't worth selling. It looks like it was a working farm once, but they're so sensitive about killing animals, I wonder how they managed. They seem to be only pretending to farm now." She retrieved her socks from where they had been warming on the radiator. Putting them on was bliss, but it never lasted long enough.

Tired of shivering and drinking hot cups of tea, they walked across the street to the pub for lunch. It felt comfortable and warm, and the food was as delicious as always. Afterwards, Andy, the bartender, smiled when they ordered a beer at the bar to delay going home for an hour or so.

He asked, "How are things going in that house across the street?" Andy was in his twenties with disheveled brown hair and an open face covered in light freckles.

Sarah said, "The house is a bit cold, but other than that, we love it here."

A couple of older men chuckled at the end of the bar. One looked over and said, "You're renting the coldest house in the village, so we knew you'd be mentioning it sooner or later."

Andy laughed, "I'm afraid it's true. I can lend you extra blankets if you need some." He poured two more pints of Guinness. "These two are on me."

Tom took a sip of the creamy foam on top. "Don't worry, we don't need a thing. The Hambys left us more firewood and blankets than we could ever use. Now that we know it's famous, we won't feel like such American wimps sleeping in our hats and our socks."

Andy said, "I've known the Hambys all my life. There are no better people anywhere."

Sarah agreed, "They're perfect landlords, and Nicola is such a good cook. We're always excited when she invites us to dinner."

Before they left, the two older men recommended buying hot water bottles and tried to send them a third pint of Guinness, but Tom asked for a raincheck.

~~

Signs of the holiday season started appearing halfway through December. It was a much less commercial affair than in America, made evident only by sprigs of holly and Christmas cake on offer in the tea shops. Sarah and Tom both had to work on Christmas day, but they were able to join the Hambys for the town's traditional celebration at the Village Hall on Christmas Eve.

When they arrived, there were already dozens of people seated at the white plastic tables. The food table had a red paper tablecloth with smiling cardboard Santa Claus faces taped to the corners and the catering was perfunctory: mixed nuts, mince pies, a big plate of store-bought shortbread cookies with coffee, tea, hot cider, and Styrofoam cups.

Nicola and John chatted with the neighbors, Audrey talked with the other teenagers, and Sam hovered over the cookies. Sarah and Tom met a few new people, but the whole thing struck Sarah as being sad rather than joyous. Tom put a few snacks on a small paper plate, and they wandered over to a table. The Hamby family soon joined them.

John settled in beside Sam and said, "We're going on holiday in Italy on Boxing Day. It's our first one in quite a long time."

Sarah took a bite of the small mince pie and caught the crumbling pastry before it hit the floor. "That's great!" she said.

Nicola smiled, "You may change your mind when you hear the favor we need to ask you. By the way, Boxing Day is the day after Christmas. It's great fun at the pub across the street."

Tom said, "Ask us anything and we'll do it."

John said, "We have a new young pig who needs feeding while we're gone. She's the apple of Sam's eye so we want to leave her in good hands while we're away. It's too cold outside now, so she'll be staying in the barn until spring, and it's right next door to your house. She loves people and has lots of personality. Her name is Shirley."

Tom said, "Yes sir. We'll be happy to feed Shirley and keep her company while you're in Italy." He gave Sam a thumbs-up.

Audrey had brought a small battery-powered electric keyboard from the Hamby house. When they finished their snacks, she placed it on the table and played Christmas carols with one finger, and Sam sang *Away in a Manger* at the top of his lungs drowning out all the other people in the room. Sarah thought it was hilarious but when she glanced at Nicola, there was a tear running down her face.

Later that evening, Sarah and Tom climbed under the heavy blankets and admired each other's sleeping hats. It was so cold that Sarah saw Tom's breath when he was laughing.

She said, "I dread tomorrow."

Tom put his arm around her, "I know it's a drag. It should have been our first Christmas together and instead we're both working."

"I'll miss you, but it's not just that. I'm supposed to induce labor and perform a breech delivery tomorrow. The baby has its rear end down instead of its head, and we're giving the patient medicine to start contractions. It seems risky to me, but every time I refuse to do something, someone asks, "And you say you're fully trained in America?"

Tom said, "You're better than fully trained. You should do what you think is right."

"Oddly enough, it's hard to know what's right. We usually deliver breeches by C-section in America. The two countries do things so differently that I'm beginning to wonder how much of medicine is science and how much is superstition. I plan to proceed with caution and do a C-section at the slightest sign of a problem."

"I know you'll do the right thing. You're a great doctor," Tom cuddled up behind her and nestled his face in her back. It felt so reassuring she fell asleep within minutes.

The next morning, she started her rounds on the obstetrics ward and was introduced to the patient with the breech presentation by Valerie, the midwife in charge of her care. Sarah was glad it was Valerie because she was one of the more experienced midwives on the unit.

The patient, Mrs. Thomas, nodded while Sarah sat by the bedside and explained the procedure for starting the contractions. She already appeared tired and listless. It was her first pregnancy, and judging from the lack of smiles, it didn't look as if it had been an easy one. Sarah hoped Valerie would be able to cheer her up a little.

At noon, a group of senior doctors, including Mr. Adam, arrived dressed in Santa Claus hats. They visited all the wards and carved turkeys, filling plates with mashed potatoes, bread sauce, and Brussels sprouts. The Sister told her it was a British tradition. Sarah couldn't imagine doctors in America interrupting their holiday to serve Christmas dinner to hospital patients.

She went to the labor ward several times during the day, and Valerie was happy to report good progress with the contractions. Mrs. Thomas was more talkative but still had no questions. In England, women rarely had any questions after Sarah's lengthy explanations of options and treatment. She never expected she would be waxing nostalgic for her patients in New York, who'd asked too many questions.

The thing she really missed about America was the personal nature of the care. In England, she was responsible for so many patients that it was hard to develop relationships with them. At its worst, the public system was run like a factory with everything done for expediency's sake. She wondered if they delivered breeches vaginally in Britain because they didn't want to add more C-sections to an elective surgery schedule that was already overloaded and had waiting lists.

Back in the call room, she sat on the bed and ate a turkey sandwich for supper. The room was as claustrophobic as most of the call rooms she'd encountered in her career. On Christmas Day, it felt even more depressing.

At eight o'clock Valerie called and said that Mrs. Thomas was fully dilated. Since her contractions had slowed, Valerie wanted to increase the medicine to speed them up. Sarah disagreed. She mentioned the possibility of a C-section, but Valerie was sure the patient could deliver vaginally.

At ten o'clock, after Mrs. Thomas had pushed for two hours, Valerie called Sarah for the delivery. Sarah gowned and gloved then prepped and draped the patient. She sat on a stool and watched as Mrs. Thomas pushed. After another fifteen minutes of pushing, she turned to Valerie and said, "This baby's not coming down. Can you call the surgical crew for a C-section?"

Valerie made the call then walked over to Sarah and said, "They're tied up right now for another half hour or so. I think she can do it. Let's give her a little longer."

Sarah said, "All right, but not too much longer."

With Valerie urging her on, the patient increased her efforts. Ten minutes later, Sarah decided it was time for the delivery. She told Valerie to call the pediatric doctor. After the call was made, she numbed the vagina and made an incision.

Despite the generous episiotomy, the baby didn't move down much more with the next few pushes, and now the baby had descended too far to do a C-section.

Sarah had delivered a few breeches vaginally, although it was rarely done in American hospitals. She knew it was important not to pull too much on the body, and she was able to get the baby halfway out without much pulling. But after that, the baby got stuck and no matter what maneuver she tried, she couldn't free up the arms and deliver the head.

As one attempt after the other failed, she was aware of additional seconds passing by with no oxygen to the baby. The Pediatric doctor was hovering over her shoulder. Both of them knew it was taking much too long.

When she was finally able to complete the delivery a few minutes later, the baby boy was dead. It was too late for Pediatrics to save it.

Sarah was devastated. Nothing like this had ever happened to her before. One of the things that distressed her most was Mrs. Thomas's quiet resignation when Sarah explained to her what happened. Instead of blaming Sarah, she turned her face away to hide her tears.

After a sleepless night in the call room and a difficult drive home the next morning, Sarah started to sob as soon as she walked in the door. Tom came running down the stairs when he heard her.

"My God, what happened?" He put his arms around her, and she cried on his shoulder.

"The baby died," she said.

"Which baby?"

"They wouldn't let me do the C-section when I needed to, and he got stuck. I killed him."

"You did not. It sounds like you tried to do the right thing." Tom grabbed a box of tissues and led her over to the sofa.

She said, "The right thing would've been to stop and wait for the surgical crew no matter how close she was to a vaginal delivery. He'd still be alive and she'd have her baby in her arms if I'd done what I really thought was right." She looked down in shame.

Tom massaged her back and said, "You're a good doctor, Sarah. Everybody loves you."

"No, I'm not a good doctor. I just lost a baby. It didn't have to happen."

Sarah trudged upstairs to take a bath, and Tom cooked some oatmeal for breakfast. After they finished eating, she told him she wanted to sleep all day. She couldn't bear to be with anyone, not even Tom, so she made him promise to go to the pub in the afternoon to see what Boxing Day was all about.

The next day it was hard for Sarah to get out of bed. It had been impossible to sleep more than a couple of hours or eat more than a few bites of food, so her heart raced every time she stood up. She was relieved to have a few days off for the holidays because the thought of going back to the hospital was so depressing. She also needed more time to figure out how to stop crying.

Tom brought meals in, but otherwise left Sarah alone to recover. He convinced her to walk with him to feed Shirley the pig around noon. It took a few minutes for Sarah's eyes to adjust to the darkness when they walked inside the barn. Shirley jumped up and grunted as soon as she saw them from her enclosure.

Shirley reminded Sarah of an English bulldog, but she had a much happier face. Also, she didn't feel anything like a dog. There was nothing soft about the pig's bristly hair, and her flanks were as solid as wood. She bounded over to the feed trough when Tom poured out her pellets.

"How was Boxing Day?" Sarah sat down on the stacked feedbags in the corner.

"Pretty raucous. Everybody ate big roast beef sandwiches, and these guys that looked like Rugby players drank lots of beer and sang Christmas carols. They were so loud you could barely hear yourself talk."

"Sam sang loudly like that at the Village Hall so maybe it's a custom around here. By the way, have you ever thought there was something sad about the Hambys?"

"Why do you ask?" Tom grabbed the hose and topped up Shirley's water.

"Because I saw Nicola cry that night and I wondered why."

"Maybe they're sad they can't run the farm properly. What could they be planning to do with this pig?" Tom shoveled out her litter and replaced it with fresh straw.

"She's pretty cute." Sarah felt Shirley's ears. They weren't soft, either.

"We had pigs on our farm. They're a handful when they're older. There's no sense in having them except to butcher, and you know that's not going to happen." Tom looked down at Shirley with disdain.

Sarah stood up. "You'd be happy if all the animals here were slaughtered."

Tom said, "Sarah, this isn't a farm, it's a petting zoo."

In early March, signs of spring began to break the tedium of the winter. Daffodils bloomed by the river, and small patches of bluebells appeared on the edge of the fields. Sarah's mood had been glum since Christmas, but the occasional day of sunshine lifted her spirits a little.

The Hambys finally let Shirley out of the barn into the field after her winter of darkness. She played with Sam in the bright sunlight, running, jumping, and rolling in the grass. Sarah had never seen an animal so joyful.

By the end of March, Sarah was exhausted from the strain of the English system with too few doctors for too many patients and Tom felt he'd learned as much as he could about English cuisine. They decided to leave England in May, which was four months earlier than they'd originally planned. They both found jobs in New Mexico.

At breakfast one sunny morning in April, they finally felt the house getting warmer inside. Tom buttered his toast and added some bitter orange marmalade.

He said, "The chef at the restaurant told me there was a farm near us that butchered great lamb for Easter."

Sarah said, "I'm not sure I want lamb for Easter."

Tom smiled, "It's our last chance for English lamb. I was looking forward to cooking it."

She took a sip of tea, "I've been feeling less and less like eating animals lately. I'm sorry, but even the smell of lamb cooking might turn my stomach."

A WINTER IN SOMERSET

"As I remember, you were the one who made the most fun of the Americans who ran away when the Navajo killed the sheep for the barbecue. You accused them of being wimps and anthropomorphizing. The Hambys must have worn off on you."

Sarah poured another cup of tea and said, "I don't know, but let's make a deal. We'll go to the pub one last time for Easter. You can have the lamb, and I'll have a lovely jacket potato."

Tom figured the pub would also be serving local lamb, so he was happy enough to agree.

Sarah and Tom slept late on Easter Sunday and went to the pub around noon. When they finished their meal, they wandered to the bar to have one last Guinness and say goodbye to Andy.

Andy exclaimed, "My favorite two customers! Is that house still cold across the street?"

Tom said, "No, it's much better. It makes it even sadder that it's time for us to go back to America."

Andy poured them some Guinness from the tap, "You can't be leaving already. You just got here."

Sarah said, "We're going back next week. I can't believe it's our last time here. We'll miss you!"

"I'll miss you too." Andy said. "I know the Hambys will miss you most of all. Having you around really cheered them up after the tragedy they'd been through."

Sarah asked, "What tragedy? We don't know about it."

Andy pulled his stool over, sat down in front of them, and spoke softly, "They lost a child a couple of years before you came. It was sad for the whole village."

Tom asked, "Oh no, what happened?"

"Their child, Tim, was only a bit older than three when it happened. He was as cute as a button. He wandered out of the house one morning to watch John working on the tractor, but John didn't know he was there. He was moving big bales of hay, and one of them dropped on top of Tim. By the time they realized it, it was too late."

Sarah put her face in her hands, "They never mentioned it. We had no idea what they'd been through."

Andy said, "They've never talked about it much, but I think it weighs heavily on their hearts."

Tom put his hand over Sarah's on the bar and said, "I guess there was something sad about the Hambys, after all."

Sarah said, "They figured out a way to have a farm without death, by not killing any animals. Maybe all farms should be petting zoos instead."

ROCK WITH WINGS

After a decade of searching New York City for the right job and a good apartment, Caroline found both in the same year. She moved into the third floor of a brownstone on the West Side less than ten blocks from where she worked. She was relieved the apartment hadn't exhibited any fatal flaws yet. As far as she could tell, it had adequate heat, a working stove, no bedbugs, and no restless drug addicts on the floor above.

She'd moved to New York in her early twenties after getting a master's degree in social work. It was the perfect place to get her feet wet, but she never expected to stay well into her thirties. She did know that once she left her family and hometown in Georgia, she was probably never coming back. Part of New York City's charm was having no requirement that the residents fit in. In fact, it seemed to encourage the opposite.

There were still a few boxes to unpack in the bedroom. In one, she found the carefully packed remnants of a trip during college. She cleared off the top of her bookcase so she could put them in their usual place.

Despite her caution while removing the tissue paper from the gnarled branch, a few more of the spiky leaves fell off. She placed the branch carefully at the back edge of the bookcase. Next, she unwrapped a triangular piece of broken pottery as large as the palm of her hand. It was a dull grey color and had ridges that must have run horizontally across the pot. She touched the fingerprints around the rim and put it in front so the light hit the ridges and she would be able to see it from her bed.

The next thing was a silver bear claw necklace still on its black velvet pad looking just the same as when she'd bought it ten years ago. She propped it against the bottom of the branch. Lastly, she brought out a foot-long pink bull on his rough wooden pedestal, an elongated animal with tiny horns and hooves. His face had shiny black eyes and a black wool thread that curved into a smile. His body was covered in bright pink fabric on top with a white stomach below. She stood him up in the middle of her bookshelf display.

She carried these things with her from place to place, and they'd been unpacked in six New York apartments now. It wasn't because they made her feel happy or peaceful. In fact, it was the opposite. After ten years, they still left her feeling guilty and sad. Her hope was that having them physically present might help her understand things one day.

~~

When she was in her last year of college, Caroline signed up for the Navajo Immersion Project. As advertised, it was the most significant week of her life.

The first morning on the reservation, Caroline didn't know where she was when she woke up. The room was small and unfamiliar, and the window at the foot of the bed was too streaked and milky to offer any more clues. She raised herself on her elbows and remembered that she was in a trailer in a town called Shiprock in the Navajo Nation, a country within her country.

When she got up and opened the window to look outside, the desert stretched out as far as she could see. A pack of skinny dogs wandered by. They ranged in size from a Dachshund to a German Shepherd. Some even looked like a crossbreed between the two. She closed the window and looked around the room. Everything was coated in sand, and the small stove in the kitchen was covered in grease that smelled of bacon.

The shower was only a trickle of cold water, but she managed to wash her hair. She was supposed to meet the project leader at the Navajo Community College. After walking around the neighborhood twice, she finally managed to find the sign and the two-storied blue paneled building.

She realized she was starving. There was no store or restaurant close-by, or even a gas station in sight, just two lines of identical cement block houses with sandy yards and tall weeds along the fences. Sadly, Tony Begay, the project manager, had no coffee or food when she found his office on the second floor.

Tony was tall with a straw cowboy hat and a rodeo belt buckle as big as a saucer. He spoke softly and so slowly it was hard to know when his sentences ended. He handed her a list of Navajo words, and they went over them together.

She learned that the Navajo were called *Dine'* or the people, and she was an Anglo or a *Bilagáana*. He laughed when she had some success with mimicking the prolonged vowels and guttural endings and said she must have Navajo ancestors. He told her that Ruth, her *Bilagáana* partner, would be arriving at noon tomorrow then he would take them to their family, a grandmother and her daughter in Two Grey Hills at the foot of the Lukachukai Mountains.

When she finally had the nerve to ask about food, he said he'd totally forgotten. They got in his pick-up and drove down to the Saturday market in Shiprock. His truck was twenty years old, but meticulously clean inside.

The town was named Shiprock because of a massive volcanic core that resembled a ship floating on the flat desert sands. Tony said the Navajo called it the 'Rock with Wings' or *Tsé Bit' A'í*. Caroline didn't have as much luck pronouncing that. When she said the Shiprock looked ghostly and mysterious, he said everyone who touched the rock had died.

It felt like a foreign country as she walked beside Tony through the Navajo market. It was held where the two main highways crossed, in a large lot full of white plastic tables and pickup trucks. A cloud of dust and smoke from cedar fires hung over the area. The smell of dough frying and meat cooking made Caroline's mouth water.

Tony took her to a stall where they were making Navajo tacos. He bought two coffees, handed her one, and chatted in Navajo with the women cooking the food. Everyone in the market seemed to know and like Tony. Caroline wished she could understand what he was saying because he had the women in fits of laughter.

Since she couldn't participate in the conversation, she wandered over to look at a few tables and sipped the bitter coffee from the white Styrofoam cup. She didn't expect the coffee to be so strong and was sorry she'd been too shy to ask for milk and sugar.

An interesting assortment of melons, corn, squash, piñón nuts, tomahawks, moccasins, puppies, baby chicks, feathered dreamcatchers, bow and arrow sets, and silver jewelry was for sale.

Most of the Navajo women were traditionally dressed in long gathered skirts, velvet blouses, and elaborate turquoise squash blossom necklaces. Everything was from another era except their dusty tennis shoes. The men looked like Tony with cowboy hats, jeans, rodeo buckles, and practical cowboy boots. When Caroline asked an older woman about a necklace on her table, she remained silent and pointed at the price in reply.

Tony called her over when the tacos were ready and refused to let her pay him for the food. They sat in the shade of a tree on folding chairs and balanced the paper plates on their laps. The taco was a plate-sized piece of freshly fried dough piled with spicy meat, beans, lettuce, tomato, and cheese with a dollop of sour cream on top. Caroline ate half and replaced the foil on the other half for later. She didn't know when she was going to get more food.

After they finished, she took Tony over to the woman selling the necklace so she could ask some questions. The older woman smiled when she saw Tony as if she knew him.

Caroline said, "Can you ask her if this necklace was made by someone who lives around here?" She pointed to the necklace she'd been looking at earlier.

Tony turned to the woman. They had a long exchange with many pauses.

He finally nodded his head and said to Caroline, "Her cousin made it."

Caroline waited for more information, but Tony was silent. She asked, "What kind of animal claw is that engraved in the silver?" She picked it up to look at it more closely.

Tony said, "It's a bear claw. Bears have healing power in Navajo culture. They guide our spirits." He took the necklace from Caroline and turned it in the sunlight to inspect the engraving.

The price was too high for Caroline, and she decided not to risk insulting the woman by trying to bargain. She thanked Tony for his help and turned away, but the woman interrupted and spoke to him with some urgency.

Tony said, "She'd like for you to have it."

Caroline said, "I don't think I can afford it."

The woman and Tony had another long conversation. They both looked serious.

He said to Caroline, "She says wearing it will protect you. She can see the future and thinks you'll need it very soon. It would mean a lot to her to know she's helped you."

Caroline emptied her wallet to pay for the necklace, and Tony fastened it around her neck in case she needed the protection immediately.

All these years later, Caroline clearly remembered buying the necklace because she couldn't afford it and hadn't even liked it that much.

~~

Not speaking up had always been a problem for Caroline. She'd been unusually quiet, even as a young child. She felt like an alien alongside her two vivacious blonde sisters and perfectly groomed mother, who all enjoyed putting on the Southern charm. She was big boned and serious like her father, a Yankee from the North, and had his dark unruly hair and intense brown eyes.

She'd chosen to go to college in Arizona to get as far away as possible from her home in Athens, Georgia. Unfortunately, Phoenix had the same brand of co-eds wandering the streets as the university town she came from. She avoided the sororities, made friends with a couple of shy students she met at the laundromat, and studied social work. She even lost her Southern accent.

She heard about the Navajo Immersion Project from one of her teachers. It was begun in the late 1980's with students from Arizona State University. The plan was for social work students to live with a Navajo family for a week in the summer and actually experience the physical conditions of the culture. Dr. Freeman, her instructor, described it as 'learning by doing'; education provided by reality instead of books.

Reality set in when Tony took her by the Thriftway gas station on the way back, so she could pick up something to eat for the next morning. She found a package of tea bags and a sweet roll in a cellophane package smudged with icing. By the time he dropped her off at the trailer, the meat juice from the Navajo taco plate in her lap had leaked all over her pants. Besides washing her clothes in the sink, she wondered what she was going to do for the rest of the afternoon.

By the time Tony reappeared with Ruth the next day, she'd finished reading the only book she'd brought with her, an autobiography of a Navajo man named Left Handed who'd lived in the late 1800's. She particularly liked his name and the book title: *Son of Old Man Hat*. This time she told Tony right away that she was hungry.

Ruth was a tall athletic looking girl who had grown up on a horse farm in El Paso. She had a Texas twang and a practical air about her. She told Tony that the only indigenous people she'd known growing up were from Mexico. That was one step ahead of Caroline who'd never heard of anyone with Native American blood in Athens, Georgia.

The three of them got in the front seat of his pickup. Caroline sat in the middle with her knees to one side so Tony could change the gears. He took them to a restaurant a couple of miles down the road named *Chat n Chew*, and they all had big plates of hamburgers with French fries and lots of ketchup. The diner was just as meticulously clean as Tony's pickup. One of the workers mopped under all the vacant tables while they ate and stood nearby with the bucket waiting for them to leave.

When they finished eating, Tony said, "We can go to the grocery store before we drive to your family. They'll feed you the main meals, but you might want to buy some snacks."

As they walked out, Caroline looked back to observe the guy move in with the mop.

Caroline still recalled how embarrassed she felt that day for insisting on a separate grocery cart to carry all the food she needed. But if the last two days had been any indication of the week ahead, she wanted to be prepared. The food Ruth put in her cart looked paltry by comparison.

Tony needed to buy *ach'íí*, so Caroline and Ruth wheeled their carts behind his to the butcher section. He found it in a display case full of organ meat and slabs of fat. Caroline recognized the liver and kidneys from biology class, but the *ach'íí* didn't look like any organ she'd studied so she asked him what it was.

"It's sheep intestines wound around a piece of fat," he said. "It's really good when you fry it up."

Caroline and Ruth exchanged worried glances. Both of them grabbed more cookies and chips on the way out the door.

It took thirty minutes to get to the turning for Two Grey Hills. After driving through a couple of housing projects near town, the land was totally deserted. Rust-colored sand and dark rocks of all sizes stretched out on either side. The road passed close to the Shiprock on the way. Caroline and Ruth leaned out the windows as they drove by, then turned around to watch it receding in the distance. It looked otherworldly and strange.

Tony said, "The Rock with Wings or Shiprock, the *Bilagáana* name, is sacred. It's the great bird that carried our people here from the cold lands in the north long ago. The bird was injured during a battle and turned to stone."

When they passed another large volcanic rock closer to the road, Caroline asked, "What's this rock called?"

Tony said, "Bennett Peak. It's where all the Skinwalkers are."

Ruth asked, "What's a Skinwalker?"

"They're witches in animal skins that can curse you or play tricks on you. You can always tell when they're near because they smell like dead animals. They're not alive, but they're not dead either." Tony's mood was no longer lighthearted.

There was silence for a while afterwards. After they made the turn, Tony suggested they practice their Navajo. The road was much smaller with lots of steep curves as it wound its way up the hill. There started to be signs of plant life, tall clumps of grass and brittle bushes, and large hills visible in the distance. Caroline noticed the carcass of a dead dog on the shoulder.

Tony said, "When we get there, the grandmother, Roberta, will be by herself because her daughter Annie works at the hospital all day. Roberta doesn't speak English. When you meet her, you should shake her hand and say *Yá'át'ééh shimá*. It means 'Hello, Grandmother.'"

Both Ruth and Caroline lowered their voices and slowly repeated 'Yah tey shma'.

He said, "The grandmother is the head of the family. She's the boss and lives in her own place on the property. Her land is passed on to her daughter, so the families always live where she lives and belong to the same clan."

He added, "Another good word to learn is the one for thank you. It's *ahéhee'*"

When Ruth said 'A yeh heh' with her Texas accent, he laughed and said, "I guess that'll work." Caroline was too shy to give it a try after Ruth had mangled it.

They rounded a particularly sharp bend and turned onto a dirt road marked by two stacked truck tires. The dirt road headed straight to the foot of the larger hills. After about a mile, they reached a small house with a round wooden structure in front of it that Tony said was a hogan, the traditional grandmother's house. It had a mud roof, a single door, and no windows.

The yard was full of wandering sheep and three dogs bounded up to the truck. A yellow horse stood in a small corral out back.

Tony knocked softly and greeted Roberta warmly when she came to the door. She smiled when Caroline and Ruth shook her hand and motioned for them all to come inside. The hogan had a dirt floor and was like a log cabin on the inside with an intricate ceiling and vertical logs forming the interior walls. There was a beautiful rug at the entrance and a brightly colored blanket on the single bed in the back. Tony said Two Grey Hills was famous for its weavers.

The wood stove in the middle had a fire in it and was putting out heat, which puzzled Caroline since it was summer. They sat around a small table and Roberta poured coffee into four blue enamel cups. It had the same bitter taste as the coffee at the Shiprock market.

Roberta was traditionally dressed in a dark red velvet top and a pink gathered skirt, and her hair was pulled back with white wool wound around it. She spoke to Tony like an old friend and seemed to be kidding him about something. Caroline took off her jacket and nursed the coffee. Ruth looked around like she'd landed on Mars.

Afterwards, Tony showed them Annie's house where they'd be staying, a simple cement block house with two bedrooms and a working bathroom. He helped them carry all their groceries inside and told them he'd be back on Friday. He beeped the horn as he drove away.

Caroline and Ruth's bedroom had two single beds that had been neatly made up, a dresser with a mirror, and a small closet. They felt guilty about crowding Annie's kitchen with their junk food, so they stacked it on the shelves in the closet.

Ruth sat on her bed and started unpacking her suitcase. She said, "The Skinwalkers sound pretty scary. I hope there aren't any around here."

Caroline was trying to find space in the closet now that all the shelves were full of food. "I was expecting peace and harmony, but I guess every culture has its superstitions. My mother thinks that if we don't eat black-eyed peas on New Year's Day, we'll have bad luck all year."

Ruth said, "Mine too!"

Caroline gave up on the closet, repacked her suitcase, and slid it under the bed. "I'm more like my father. He's a science professor and doesn't buy into that kind of stuff." She handed Ruth her book, *Son of Old Man Hat*. "This book really helped me understand some things. I've finished, so you can have it."

Ruth looked at the photograph of the traditional Navajo man on the cover.

Caroline said, "A person has many mothers in the Navajo culture. There's your birth mother and then all the other mothers who help take care of you. I think that's why we call Roberta 'Grandmother', even though we're not related."

Annie came home at five. She was wearing a nurse's uniform with white tennis shoes. Her long hair was tucked behind her ears. She wore glasses and had a big smile. Caroline and Ruth were both happy to hear they were having Navajo Tacos for dinner.

She peeked in their room and said, "You're staying in the room where my two daughters grew up. They've both got their own children now. One's in Phoenix and the other's in Farmington. My husband's gone. He married another woman after me."

Annie looked about forty so Caroline concluded that their generations must still be quite short. In *Son of Old Man Hat*, pregnancy was encouraged soon after puberty.

When Roberta walked in a few minutes later, Annie greeted her with respect. Ruth and Caroline helped set the table, and everyone remained quiet while they were eating.

Caroline was starting to feel uncomfortable, until Ruth broke the silence saying, "These tacos taste so good I wish we could have them every night!"

Annie and Roberta spoke in Navajo for a little while and Annie said, "Mom makes fry bread every morning, so we can. Tomorrow you'll get a special treat though. It's the corn harvest so she's making Kneeldown bread and mutton stew."

Roberta smiled proudly. She talked to Annie and nodded towards Ruth and Caroline.

Annie said, "She says you can help with the sheep. She'll go with you to check on them in the morning tomorrow and then you can go see them again before the sun goes down. The dogs are the ones that mostly protect them out there."

In the morning, Annie walked behind the house to show them the well and how to use its pump before she left. She said the water was safe to drink for animals and for people.

Roberta came out of her hogan and called the black and white collie dog that slept close to her door. She led the yellow horse out with a halter, threw a blanket across her back, and stood on a stump to mount her. The spotted dog took the lead, and Caroline and Ruth walked along behind Roberta and the horse.

On the way Roberta was silent, so they were silent too. It was a couple of miles before they found the sheep. Roberta rode across the area where the sheep were grazing and looked down at the various grasses. Caroline and Ruth cautiously moved through the flock wondering what they should do. After quiet consultation, they decided counting the sheep twice daily would be their most important task. Caroline still remembered that there were twenty-three of them.

By the time they got back, they were both sunburned. Roberta shook their hands, said *ahéhee'*, and disappeared into her hogan. They opened all the windows in Annie's house, but it was still hot inside because there was no air conditioning. They took two cold Cokes and some chips and onion dip and sat in the shade of a large umbrella-shaped tree between the two houses for the rest of the afternoon.

When Annie got home, she said, "I see you found the Navajo willow. It's lots cooler out here than in the house this time of day."

Ruth asked Annie, "When should we go check on the sheep again?"

She said, "Now would be a good time."

Ruth looked over to the corral. "Can we take the horse?"

Annie walked over to the corral and picked up the halter and blanket, "Sure. She's real gentle. We've had her for fifteen years."

Ruth clipped the halter on her, "I know she's quiet, since this halter is all she needs."

Annie nodded and said, "She's never had a bit in her mouth."

Caroline called across the yard to the dog, "Cha, come and help us find the sheep!"

This made Annie laugh so hard she had to hold on to the post to stay standing.

Caroline felt embarrassed. She said, "I thought that was what he was called."

"*Chaa* means poop in Navajo. A dog is a *lii chaa*. That's what Mom calls him. Instead of poop, it means poop-eater. I guess it's not much better, but it's what dogs do."

Lii chaa found the flock easily. The two guard dogs had led the sheep to a small pond for water. There were still twenty-three sheep, and Ruth let Caroline ride the horse on the way back. Caroline was glad of Ruth's practical experience in the country and around horses. She couldn't imagine what the week would have been like without her.

The mutton stew that night was thin without much meat or salt, but the Kneeldown bread, wrapped in corn husks, was delicious. Ruth said it tasted like sweet tamales.

The next morning it rained. The windows were open, and Caroline could smell wet sand and another strong fragrance, similar to eucalyptus, coming in from outside. It was almost dry by the time she and Ruth went out to check on the sheep. *Lii chaa* found them on a sand ridge overlooking a valley with tall trees and lots of grass.

All the dogs were playful that morning. They rolled over each other and ran in circles around the sheep. Ruth and Caroline tried to teach them to fetch sticks but had no success. The dogs enjoyed tugging but were confused when the girls threw the sticks away.

Ruth called to Caroline, "Come look! I think these are chips of flint on the ground. We should search for arrowheads up here."

They scoured the ridge for an hour and found not only flint, but pieces of pottery. Some were painted red and some were decorated along the edge with fine black lines. Ruth found a small arrowhead with the base intact and only a small section of the tip broken and quickly pocketed it. Caroline found something even better. She would never forget the moment she spotted part of a pot sticking out of the sand and dug down to find a piece as big as her hand.

She showed it to Annie when she got home from work that afternoon.

Annie said, "I found one like this once, but Mom made me throw it away because she said it was cursed. She studied it closely. "I remember now. These are all fingerprints on the ridges. They pressed the ridges together to make the pot and made a pretty pattern."

Caroline looked and saw the small round fingerprints running along every ridge. She wondered whether the pot was made by children or if an adult's hands were that small back then. It was amazing to hold something with fingerprints from fifteen hundred years ago.

Annie said, "One of our doctors has a wife who studies the old ones called the Anasazi. She says they ate people. This looks like it was a big pot. She says they boiled heads in those."

Annie said to herself. "Maybe our old people knew about it all along."

Caroline kept it anyway since the fingerprints had more meaning for her than the curse or the cannibalism.

Annie had the next day off, so she took them to see the rug weavers. When they got to the end of their dirt road, Annie sounded the horn before turning onto the paved one. She said there'd been accidents in the past because the paved road had such a steep curve right before their driveway.

They drove to a house that belonged to a famous weaver named Alice Redhorse. The one-story house was twice as big as Annie's and exactly the same beige color. When they walked inside, they found most of the house taken up by the loom.

ROCK WITH WINGS

Alice had a kind face and spoke some English. Annie said she was the same age as Roberta, her mother, but her hair was already grey. She sat at the loom and showed the girls how it worked. The wool she used was dyed in earth tones, and the rug she was finishing had grey and brown geometric shapes.

They went from there to the Two Grey Hills Trading Post, which Annie said was almost a hundred years old. There were many rugs there and beautiful pots for sale. Caroline was disappointed she couldn't buy even a small painted pot because she'd spent most of her money on the silver necklace. Ruth bought a small model of a hogan to show everyone in Texas.

~~

On their last day, Caroline and Ruth woke up a little later, and Annie had already gone to work. They ate their usual corn flakes for breakfast and walked outside. Roberta was sweeping in front of her hogan, and she waved to them from across the yard.

They both heard a noise and looked up to see a car coming down the dirt road in a cloud of dust. The beat-up grey Ford stopped short of the house, and two young men, who were about their age, got out.

The driver stumbled then stayed with the car resting his hand on the hood. The other young man walked towards where they were standing under the Navajo willow. Caroline was surprised to see Roberta go inside the hogan and slam the door.

He introduced himself as Clarence Benally and pointed at the driver and said he was his brother Harry. Clarence was striking. He had a shy smile, thick black hair, and a twinkle in his eye. He said, "We need gas money and have some Navajo stuff for sale. Maybe you'd be interested?"

Ruth said, "Sure," and they all walked over to the car.

His brother Harry was less friendly and looked worse for wear. He said hello under his breath and got back in the driver's seat. Clarence grabbed the keys from him and opened the trunk. There were all sorts of things inside.

He sorted through bunched up pieces of brightly colored cloth, hanks of wool, animal bones and deer antlers bleached white from the sun, rough wooden planks, and feathers to find three elongated bulls in yellow, pink, and blue colors, which he placed on the top of the car. He rummaged through everything again and brought out a box of painted wooden dolls he called kachinas. They were elaborately decorated and represented the gods of another tribe, the Hopi.

He was proud of the kachina dolls but wanted more money than Caroline and Ruth had left over. He said the bulls were only ten dollars, so Caroline decided to buy the pink one. She carried it inside and put it on the dresser. When she came back out, Ruth was kidding around with Clarence and Harry was asleep inside the car.

Ruth walked towards the house and met her at the Navajo willow.

She said, "These guys seem totally safe, but I think one of us should stay around if they aren't leaving. I'll check the sheep on my own and be back as soon as I can." She whistled to *Lii chaa* who was sleeping outside Roberta's door and took the horse out of the corral.

Caroline walked over to the car where Clarence was standing. She said, "The bull looks happy to have escaped the trunk. Did you make him yourself?"

He said, "I did, but they're pretty easy to make. The kids like them so Harry and I go sell them in Shiprock sometimes." He looked down shyly and kicked the dirt with his boot. "Do you have a well near here? We forgot to fill our water bottles before we left the house."

Caroline said, "It's out back and Annie said the water was good. Bring the bottles over and I'll help. It's right behind the house." She walked around to see if she still remembered how to work the pump.

After they filled four liter-sized bottles with water, Clarence said, "It's really nice back here. I like to collect things from the desert. Do you mind if I take a walk?"

Caroline said, "Not at all. Do you mind if I come along too?"

He smiled and said, "It's nice to have company for a change. I'm usually walking around all by myself."

He looked at everything along the way. He said, "See these tracks from the horse? Her feet must be tough because she's barefoot and doesn't need any horseshoes." He pointed to another set of prints, "There's a coyote that comes close to the house."

Caroline said, "I know. We hear them almost every night."

He tore a branch off a small scraggy bush, rolled the leaves around in his fingers, and held it under Caroline's nose. She said, "That's what I smelled when it rained! What is it?"

"It's sagebrush. You can always smell it when it rains out here."

Caroline took the branch from him. She asked, "Where do you live?"

Clarence said, "Right down the road. I have four brothers. Harry and I decided to be artists." He started to laugh.

"I think your art is really good," Caroline said. She looked him in the eye, so he'd know she was serious.

"I found an eagle claw holding the bottom of a sagebrush last week. I can't wait to make that into something interesting. Hey, do you want to come and look at the other stuff we've got? The house isn't too far."

"I shouldn't leave. Ruth would worry when she gets back."

"I can go get more things and bring them over here. The eagle claw is cool, and I have some other animals I'm making." Clarence started to walk back towards the house.

Caroline said, "Great! I'd love to see more of your creations." She still remembered smiling and waving to him at the door before she went inside. She put the sage branch next to the bull on the dresser.

The sound of multiple sirens started soon after Ruth got back. Caroline was worried because all the noise seemed to be coming from the end of their dirt road. They put the horse in the corral and ran down the road as quickly as they could.

They found six police cars and two ambulances at the end of the driveway. Caroline could see the grey Ford smashed almost in two between the emergency vehicles. A dented pickup truck was a little further down the road.

Ruth told Caroline to stay put and went to ask the policemen what happened. When she came back, her head hung down so low it looked like she was praying.

She said, "They both died. They made a wide turn, and the pickup came around the corner right as they pulled out. The police say they must have died right on impact, so they didn't suffer."

Caroline cried out, "It was my fault!"

Ruth put her arm around her and tried to comfort her, "It wasn't your fault. You weren't even there."

"Clarence wanted to go back to his house so he could get more of his art to show me. I should've said no. I didn't even warn him the driveway was dangerous or tell him to sound the horn before he pulled out." Caroline was sobbing like a child.

Ruth guided her back up the dirt road. "The policeman said Harry was driving."

Annie saw remnants of the accident when she returned from work. Ruth told her what had happened and took the horse out by herself to check on the sheep for the last time. Caroline realized only after she returned home that she never got to say goodbye to the guard dogs and the sheep or watch *Lii chaa* run like the wind towards the flock when he found them.

Caroline stayed in bed until dinner alternating between weeping and numbness. She came out to be polite when she heard Roberta's voice, but she didn't have any appetite. She said hello with a weak smile. Both Roberta and Annie nodded sympathetically when she sat down.

Annie said, "Caroline, you shouldn't feel bad. It wasn't your fault. Mom thought Harry had been drinking."

Caroline said, "Clarence seemed sober. He was one of the nicest people I've ever met."

Annie offered Caroline some frybread. "Clarence was always a nice kid. Harry was a mess. We have problems with alcohol out here. That's why the women always vote to make it illegal to have alcohol on the reservation."

Roberta said something to Annie who turned to Caroline and said, "Mom had ten kids, and two boys died at childbirth. There was one boy left, my brother. One night my father got drunk. He had a gun and threatened to shoot Mom. He even shot and missed once. My brother went and got the gun in his room and killed my father. We never saw my brother again after that."

Caroline wiped her tears away and said, "I'm so sorry."

Annie said, "The women are strong in this culture. We have to be."

~~

Ten years later, Caroline sat on the floor in her latest New York apartment, wadded up the newspapers, and stuffed them back into the packing boxes. She was glad to have finally found an apartment that was worthy enough to honor all her things. She was also happy to have a job at the Settlement Housing Coalition working to find affordable housing and build strong diverse neighborhoods in New York City.

She now realized that her guilt and sorrow over Clarence had darkened all her recollections of the time she'd spent on the Navajo reservation. What had stayed with her was the memory of that last day, and she hadn't remembered everything that came before.

She promised herself never to forget what a privilege it was to be welcomed into the Navajo culture by such generous people. She'd learned about life, and it continued to be the most significant week she'd ever spent.

She looked at the things on the top of the bookshelf again. The sagebrush branch would always remind her of Clarence even if it lost all its spiky sage leaves. The pink bull had gathered some dust over the years, but he was still smiling. The piece of pottery with its ancient fingerprints was probably illegal to have, but it had always made her happy.

She picked up the bear claw necklace and loosened it from the black velvet pad. She hadn't worn it since she returned from the trip ten years ago, but maybe it had protected her after all. She planned to wear it to work the next day.

FEAR NOT

NOGALES

We were married by an auto mechanic in a sandy lot full of used cars just outside of Oakland. He called his wife and son to come out of the shop when it was time for the witnesses. There was no time to plan a wedding between when we decided to marry and were due to move, so we thought it best to go it alone. There were no relatives present, no wedding rings and no photographs taken since we were both wearing old jeans. The ceremony cost twenty dollars and took ten minutes.

The next week we moved to the north coast of Devon taking only the things that fit in our two suitcases. I bought an old powder blue Mini from one of my husband's friends, and we moved into one side of an old Methodist church with a built-in lectern between the kitchen and the dining room. We'd fallen in love only a few months before, after meeting at a party in San Francisco.

My new husband was English, so he did all the driving for the first few days. I bought the Mini because I came from Tucson, which had wide straight roads. I wanted something that was not much bigger than a golf cart to get back and forth on the Beatrix Potter lanes that led from the North Devon coast to the hospital in Somerset, where I was going to work.

It was late fall and the quiet English countryside seemed like heaven. The fog lifted from the pebbled beaches in the morning as we walked through the green fields on the cliffs above them. The hedgerows had more varieties of flowers than I ever thought possible.

My final year of medical residency had included studying for the English exams and applying for positions in Britain, and I was glad to have made the effort. But as a foreigner I could only get another training position in Somerset, and I braced myself for more long hours ahead.

Everyone joked that I was moving against the tide since the English doctors dreamt of escaping the National Health System for a lucrative practice in America. No sane doctor would willingly opt for the poor pay in Britain.

My belief in free medical care for all had been reinforced by my training and fostered by my husband, Peter. He had grown up in Harrogate and got a scholarship to Eton. He then attended Sandhurst, the Royal Military Academy, and was in the British army for a few years before moving to America. He was the smartest person I had ever met.

Peter often spoke of the innate fairness of England where everyone was provided a Council flat to live in, a plot to grow vegetables in the Village Garden, and good doctors free of charge. Where the people had lived through years of rationing after the Second World War and didn't need things like sugar, ice, hot water, or clothes dryers. Where people never complained of being cold, hungry, or tired.

Medicine had helped me learn how to have a stiff upper lip, but I still felt like a spoiled American child compared to Peter. He was cheerful and considerate, no matter what happened, and thought it would be selfish to behave otherwise. I was eager to shed my American skin and not need so many things in order to be happy.

When the winter came, I was much less sure of my decision. I was spending every third night and every third weekend at the hospital as the junior doctor in charge of the Obstetrics ward. I didn't get to see the inside of the call room very much because, with eight midwives working, we were always busy.

My commute to the hospital took an hour at best. When I was home, my alarm was set for five so I could arrive in time for the morning surgeries. I learned to expect the sound of the rain in the dark when the alarm clock rang and dreaded the bitter cold of the bathroom since we couldn't afford much heat.

Peter said he knew from training troops that I hadn't nearly reached my bottom and still had plenty of reserve left to tap into. He often compared me to a good solid mare or an English sheepdog, which I hoped was a compliment. His practical experience from the army and breadth of knowledge from Eton were so impressive that I hung on his every word.

He was spending his days at home working on the book he'd always wanted to write, but he seemed to be mostly taking long walks and stopping in pubs for company. I thought his writing had real promise, so I was happy to take care of the money part. The only problem was that doctors in training were paid so little in England and we had barely enough money to get by.

One particularly miserable weekend, he left to go to a party in London and stay with some friends. I had a full schedule on Monday and stayed behind at home to get some rest. It was the first time we'd been apart since the move, so it felt strange to wake up by myself in England. On Sunday, I slept a little later than usual, and allowed myself more hot water for the bath. As I stirred my oatmeal on the stove, I noticed the mildew was covering a much bigger patch of the kitchen wall.

When I sat down on the sofa to eat, the upholstery felt damp and a musty smell wafted up. I knew nothing was going to feel clean again as long as we lived in this country. I missed the wide-open feeling of the Southwest and the clean smell of sage coming in from the desert.

In the afternoon, I put on a raincoat and went out for a walk so it would seem warmer when I came back inside. I tried to read but my hands got too cold holding the book, so I huddled by the gas stove in the blanket and watched it get dark outside. When the rain started again, I climbed into bed with my woolen socks and a flannel nightgown.

Peter felt recharged after he returned from London. He'd met a journalist at the party who wrote for the London Times, and he said she was terrific. She was interested in his writing and had lots of contacts.

"How old is she?" I asked as I brought the dinner plates to the table.

"I'd say about our age. She's not one of those frumpy, small town women you see around here. She's the best kind of

English woman," he said. He poured the Guinness in the two beer glasses.

"You mean like your sister?" I asked. Sarah, his sister, had an easy smile and was tall and hilarious.

"She's fearless like my sister, but much more interesting. She's been all over the world. In fact, she wants us to go with her on a trip to Nogales," he said.

"Nogales? Does she speak Spanish?" I watched Peter handle his knife and fork. I was still trying to perfect the two-handed British way of eating.

"No, that's why she wants to have you along. She can't wait to meet you."

When I asked how she came up with the idea of going to Nogales, he said that he'd suggested it when she said she wanted to write an article about crossing the Mexican border illegally with coyotes. He mentioned that I grew up near Nogales, and she thought it would be the perfect place for her story. He told her that I spoke Spanish and he'd been with the special forces, so we could both be useful.

"She's coming here next weekend so we can plan the trip," he said.

"My Spanish is far from fluent. Besides that, you weren't really in the special forces, were you? I asked.

He said, "If I was, I couldn't tell you." He abruptly ended the conversation, picked up the dishes, and walked around the old Methodist lectern into the kitchen.

This was a new piece of information for me, but Peter seemed to come out with new things like this all the time. I went back over the various holidays we'd taken before we were married and tried to remember any suspicious behavior. I didn't know him that well, so anything was possible.

For example, why had we visited Morocco right after America bombed Libya? And why did he take a trip alone to Colombia, where he had a friend who negotiated ransoms for kidnapped victims? I had wanted to avoid a boring life, and Peter was anything but boring. Since the truth might be hard to come by, I tried to forget about it when I could.

We met Stella at our neighborhood pub, and she was as beautiful as I had worried she would be. She had tousled blonde hair and was wearing jeans with holes in them and Australian boots. Her enthusiasm seemed genuine, and her charm was undeniable. Even with my guard up, I fell quickly under her spell. By the end of lunch, we'd planned a one-week trip to Nogales in the spring.

The fact that the plan was preposterous didn't strike me until we got home.

I asked Peter, "Why would the coyotes believe that we need to cross illegally from Mexico into America? They'll either think we're totally 'loco' or up to something shady."

We were sitting on the smelly sofa with a blanket over our legs in front of the gas heater. Peter looked up from his book and patted my leg reassuringly. He said, "My guess is they'll take our money and not ask many questions."

"Do you realize how dangerous this could be for all of us? It's a no-man's land on that border with crazy criminals and corrupt cops."

"That's why I'm along to protect you," Peter said.

"But what if there's a gang of them? What if you can't protect us?"

"Don't worry, I will," he said absentmindedly as he picked up his book and started reading again.

But I was worried. Anybody in their right mind would have been worried. Over the next few months, I tried to make my case. I told Peter I could put Stella in touch with Mexicans who had crossed the border. They could tell her their stories, and I would translate for her. That would be much more authentic than what might happen to her on the way.

He told me that articles with interviews and photographs of the Mexicans who crossed the border had already been done many times before. Stella wanted to put her life on the line just like the Mexicans did, because she was fearless and game for anything. When I reminded him that we could also be raped and killed in the process, he accused me of doubting his military experience.

In the end, I decided to go to Nogales to protect him as much as anything else. I arranged to work three additional weekends of call so I could take an extra week off. My medical skills might be needed more in Nogales than Somerset.

The dreary winter flew by because I spent so many hours at work. I put April out of my mind because I dreaded its arrival, and Peter, Stella, and I were on a plane to Nogales before I knew it. We spent the first night in a Motel 6 on the American side of the border since we were all tired from traveling. Before we went to sleep, Peter commented on how admirable it was that Stella hadn't balked at the motel because, judging from her accent, she was obviously upper class.

The next afternoon, we drove across the border and found an even worse Mexican motel, which made me happy in some twisted sort of way. We had chicken fajitas at an Applebee's in the mall next door to our hotel. It was crowded with Mexicans enthusiastically eating and carefully pronouncing the word *chicken* when they ordered.

Stella asked, "What would be a legitimate cause for us to have lost our passports?"

I said, "If we'd simply lost them, we'd deal with it through the embassies and not with the coyotes."

"We need to have had our passports revoked for some reason. The most likely cause would be a drug conviction," Peter said.

"Oh yeah, we look really likely," I said. I bore some resemblance to Julie Andrews in the Sound of Music, Stella looked like a model for Prada, and Peter had an English haircut and freckles.

Peter turned to me and said, "Like I told you, they'll take our money and won't ask many questions. I'm sure all white people look clueless to them."

FEAR NOT

I wondered where he'd come up with this idea since he didn't have any experience with Mexicans that I was aware of.

We spent the rest of the hot afternoon walking up and down the sad corridor behind the tall border fence. I translated several signs for Stella and Peter, which warned Mexicans about how dangerous it was to hire a coyote to cross the border because people often paid with their lives. They were illustrated with graveyards, but Stella and Peter seemed undeterred.

We found a good Mexican restaurant that night and drank too much at dinner. We started with Margaritas, then drank all the tempting beers sitting on ice in the stand beside our table. In the morning, even Stella looked rough.

We were so hungover we had a hard time finding our rental car in the hotel parking lot. Peter drove to an authentic looking Mexican café he'd seen on one of the main streets. It was bustling with customers and smelled of menudo. We were seated at a brightly colored table decorated with plastic flowers near the window.

Stella asked, "What's that stew that everyone is eating?"

I said, "It's menudo—a soup with bits of stomach lining floating in it. It's supposed to help with hangovers."

When she said that she wanted to order it, I tried not to wince. I had never tasted menudo—the smell was bad enough.

Peter turned to Stella and said, "I'll join you. Good old Brits. We'll try anything once."

They made a big show of eating, but I noticed neither of them finished it. Peter often lectured me about my American fear of food. He said the English were never squeamish at the table and didn't waste the parts of the animal that we refused to eat like brains, sweetbreads, and kidneys. As far as I could tell, from the hospital cafeteria, the English primarily ate 'chips' or French fries. Chips, not innards, were the core of every meal.

Our plan for the day was to explore the fence on the American side of the border in the remote places more likely to be used for crossings. It sounded less challenging than finding a coyote, which was good, because I still had a headache. As we crossed the border, I noticed that the U.S. Border Patrol had cars pulled over in several bays with leashed Rottweilers sniffing the tires.

We found a winding road that roughly followed the border with small squadrons of javelinas running across it. Stella loved the 'little piggies' as she called them. I told her they could bite, but their eyesight was poor so it was easy to get out of their way.

When we saw the border fence not too far in the distance, we decided to park the car to walk along it. As we hiked over to follow the high barbed wire fence, I looked down at Peter and Stella's shoes. Peter had on flip flops and Stella was in sandals. I reminded them to watch carefully for rattlesnakes and was glad, for once, that I had on my ratty old tennis shoes.

FEAR NOT

We walked about a mile or so and saw a dirt path on our side that led across the border to an even wider path on the other side. It traversed much less rugged country than we'd seen so far, and I noticed the fence had an opening at the bottom that might fit a person. Stella bent down to look at it more closely and before we knew it, she'd slipped through to the Mexican side. Peter took a picture of her across the border with both thumbs up. I secretly hoped it would be the only crossing we would make.

A little further down the road, we drove right through the middle of a ghost town. There were eight rickety looking buildings, some with broken windows and no doors, and there was not a soul in sight. We got out of the car to walk around, and I told Peter and Stella to watch even more carefully for rattlesnakes in the buildings, where they liked to shelter from the sun.

Since we didn't know who might be lurking, we carefully skirted the buildings. Peter thought we should look in through the back windows before entering them, even if the front door was missing.

The town did prove to be empty of people, and most of the buildings had broken glass and uninteresting trash inside. The largest building looked like it was an old hotel. Most of its windows were boarded up and the front door was locked when we tried to open it.

Peter climbed a fence in the back and managed to get in through a small window on the side. When he opened the front door to let us in, the smell was overwhelming. One corner was full of toilet paper and piles of feces and another had a huge blood stain that spread out across the floor. It was enough blood to convince me that somebody had been killed.

He said, "There are no bodies anywhere that I can see. Let's get out of here."

And we did.

Later, Peter and I were back in our room at the hotel trying to ignore the dark spots on the industrial beige carpet and endure the heat from the sun burning through the flimsy blinds.

I said, "I've had enough of this trip. Can't we go to Tucson and spend some time with my parents? I haven't seen them since we moved and it's a long time until our next trip here."

"What would Stella do? I doubt she wants to hang out with your parents. She's here to get a story. We can't bail out on her now."

Peter and my parents had only met once, so I knew he probably didn't want to hang out with them either. When they'd met before, at our house in Tucson, my father seemed skeptical, Peter seemed arrogant, and my mother was mostly silent. And Peter ranted about my parents' wanton use of ice and air conditioning as soon as we got back to the car. Since a repeat of that situation was preferable to me at the moment, I knew this trip must be pretty bad.

FEAR NOT

I said, "I get the feeling she thinks it's some grand English adventure. The people who've lost their lives on this border are just props in her story."

"That's pretty unkind. You sound like you're jealous. She's a journalist, and she's taking real risks to do her job." Peter drank half his can of Modelo in one glug. The air conditioning in our hotel only circulated hot air, and every time it turned itself on, it sounded like a jet taking off in our room.

I thought the beer would help with the heat, so I opened one too, "It's bizarre how much she enjoys taking risks. Her eyes light up when there's any hint of danger."

"I think she's fearless and daring," Peter said. What he didn't say was that he thought Americans were wimps. I'd heard him say it many times before.

"My guess is that she's been lucky so far with the risks she's taken, but one day her luck's going to run out," I said, "I don't want to be with her when that happens." I finished my Modelo and went to take a shower. For once I didn't miss the hot water.

Our plan for the third day in Nogales was to find someone who could put us in touch with a coyote and not ask why we needed one. Peter was prepared to say we'd all had convictions for illegal drugs, but I wasn't sure I could go along with a straight face because we looked so unlikely. We had breakfast at the same café. I noticed neither Stella nor Peter ordered menudo.

It was sunny and already hot outside by the time we'd finished breakfast. We decided to go back to the corridor behind the border wall and talk to anyone hanging around who looked 'dodgy'. It wasn't long before a guy approached and asked if we wanted have fun.

Despite the fact it looked like he hadn't bathed in days, Stella put her arm through his, and said, "Of course!" It was interesting to see her at work.

She chatted to him as they walked arm in arm ahead of us.

Peter nodded towards her said, "She reminds me of a thoroughbred filly."

We stopped at a stand, bought cold drinks, and sat on a bench—the only one that was vacant because it had no shade. I marveled at the fluorescent green soda Ruben had chosen for himself. Fortunately, he spoke good English, so I didn't have to translate much. I could feel my back and shoulders burning as we talked.

Peter said, "We need to find a coyote to help us cross the border."

I was amazed Ruben didn't ask why. Maybe he was too polite?

He said, "I have a friend who I think can help. He's at work today, but we could meet him tonight."

Stella batted her eyelashes, smiled, and said, "That would be amazing. Let us buy you lunch. Where's the best place around here?"

FEAR NOT

He took us inside a steamy covered market, and we sat in front of a hot cone of meat turning on a spit behind the counter. We ate tacos al pastor made with the grilled meat and pineapple salsa, which were delicious. Ruben said he would come get us at our hotel at ten o'clock that night and take us to his friend.

Peter said as we walked away, "Don't worry, I've got experience with these things. That guy is totally trustworthy." Stella wholeheartedly agreed. I guess I wasn't as 'experienced' as they were because it was hard for me to be so sure.

We went inside to nurse our sunburns and have a siesta. At dinner, I drank enough so that, for a little while, I didn't worry about following a guy we'd just met around town at night.

Ruben met us in the hotel parking lot right on time and said it was close enough to walk to see his friend. As we followed him down the dark streets, my worry returned with a vengeance. The darker it got, the more enthusiastic Peter and Stella became. I wondered who it was I'd actually married. They both seemed addicted to taking risks.

I was so relieved when we walked into a bar that I wanted to give Ruben a hug for not robbing and killing us. His friend Willy didn't look to me like the type who would know coyotes, but what did I know. We ordered beers and they put the usual extras on ice in a stand beside the table.

Stella reached across the table, put her hand on Willy's, and said, "Ruben told us you could help us cross the border with a coyote."

Weirdly enough, he also didn't ask why. Were foreigners asking for illegal crossings a common occurrence in Mexico? I'd certainly never heard of it before.

Willy was dressed in a businessman's jacket and white shirt with hair that was carefully combed and gelled. He smiled and said, "I know most about the tunnels. They're everywhere. There's probably one right under this table." Like Ruben, his English was better than I expected. I guessed it was because Nogales was a border town. I wondered how many Americans spoke good Spanish in Nogales on the other side.

"What are the tunnels like?" asked Stella.

Willy said, "I could take you to one. Most don't have lights, and they get real dark after you go in. Some connect to the sewer, so they have big rats." Ruben nodded in agreement.

I realized I needed to use the bathroom after all the beer, so Ruben pointed me in the right direction. On the way there, I noticed a table of women sitting under a bilingual sign with surprisingly cheap prices for blow jobs and sex. One of them had gone into the bathroom and was washing her underwear in the sink when I came in. She was heavily made up and her flesh was bulging out of her skimpy clothes. She gave me a friendly smile before I walked in the stall.

When I got back to the table, there was more talk of tunnels, but it was clear that Willy didn't know any coyotes. I thanked my lucky stars that Stella didn't want to go exploring the tunnels. She was deathly afraid of rats.

FEAR NOT

Ruben stayed behind with Willy. Since Peter hadn't paid much attention to the route on the way there, I had to find the way back to the hotel. We made it safely, but I was walking so fast I was almost running.

Ruben dropped by when we were having breakfast in the café the next morning. We hadn't arranged to meet, but I guess Nogales was so small, there weren't many places we could be. He said he was broke and needed money to pay back some friends. We pooled together our Mexican money, but it didn't amount to much since we had planned to get more pesos later in the day.

We checked out of our hotel and decided to drive to the part of town closest to the border. Stella was just as sunburned as we were, and she wanted to avoid walking, as much as possible, with her delicate English skin. We'd just found a place to park on a busy street when Stella bolted out of the backseat and ran down an alleyway. Peter and I jumped out quickly and ran to catch up. We saw her talking to Willy on the corner. He shook her hand and walked away before we got there.

"What was that about?" Peter asked.

"I saw him walk by and thought I'd ask one last time if he could help. We're running out of options and it's our last day," Stella said.

Since I was excited that we were running out of time, I offered no suggestions. I wondered if either of them had a clue about what they were doing.

Peter puffed himself up and said, "Don't worry. I'll take care of this. Why don't you two go and look around the shops and meet me back here in an hour?"

We bought some painted plates and copper platters in the shops and met Peter on the corner an hour later. He said, "Follow me. We need to get there quickly so I don't have time to answer questions."

He ducked into the covered market and wound his way to the very back. As we walked behind him, I tried to imagine how plausible two sunburned white women in their thirties with shopping bags would appear to a real coyote. We entered a leather stall filled with belts and bolo ties. Peter introduced us to two guys who were the opposite of reassuring. Hector had a big scar across his cheek and Luis had uncombed hair and a pockmarked face. Since Luis did most of the talking, I assumed he had more English.

He said, "We can take you across the border, but it's going to be hot." He held up a liter bottle of cloudy liquid. "We'll have plenty of water though."

I saw Stella rummaging through her pocketbook. When I heard a crinkling noise and a snap, I abruptly stood up to distract Luis who was looking in her direction. I wondered if he also knew she had removed the cellophane and popped a cassette tape into a recorder.

He shook his head and continued, "We may have to put you in a building when we're halfway there so we can check things out to be sure it's safe before we cross. You shouldn't have to wait much more than an hour. Then we can all go across."

When Peter said, "That sounds fine," I started to feel faint, so I sat down on the cool cement floor.

Luis asked, "What's the matter with her?"

I was hyperventilating and couldn't answer, so Peter said, "She'll be okay in a minute."

He asked Luis, "How much will it cost?"

"Five hundred dollars a piece, so we'll need fifteen hundred."

Peter said, "We don't have that much cash, so we'll need to figure it out."

I managed to stand up, grab my shopping bag, and was heading out the stall when I heard Luis say, "We'll come with you."

I heard Peter mumble, "That won't be necessary," and the three of us walked rapidly toward the daylight. When we finally got to the street and started sprinting, I was still afraid to look around. I was out of breath when I asked Peter, "Are they behind us?"

He said, "It's hard to tell, but I think not. Hey, isn't that the space where our car was parked next to the alleyway?"

I looked. It definitely was the space, and it was definitely not our car.

Peter patted his pockets. "Wait! I don't have my keys! I must have left them in the ignition when Stella ran down the alley. Someone stole our car!"

I scanned the streets carefully for any sign of Luis or Hector now that we were stranded. I also checked to make sure I had everything I needed in my purse. They were all there—my passport, my wallet, and my phone.

"Oh my God," Peter said, "I left my passport in the car."

Stella meekly admitted, "I did too."

Why did they leave their passports in the car? Or the keys for that matter? If Peter was in the special forces and Stella had traveled all over the world, they must have both had super competent personal assistants.

After walking miles in the sun and me asking lots of questions, we finally found the police station close to the border. With my limited Spanish, I reported the car missing and filled out many forms. It was Saturday, and we looked up the hours and found the British embassy was closed until Monday. Our flights were scheduled on Sunday, so it seemed doubtful we would make them.

When we got back out on the street, I suggested stopping at a nearby restaurant to discuss what we should do. I had a blister from my tennis shoes that was killing me, and my shoulders were an alarming shade of puce. The cold Coca-Cola there was the best thing I had ever tasted.

Stella said, "This really puts us to the test. I think we press on to find a coyote. Those two guys obviously weren't the answer. Now we *have* to do it. It's live or die."

FEAR NOT

"It didn't take me very long to find them," Peter said, "I know where to look now. It would be an even more amazing story if we get across the border in time to make our flight."

I asked the waitress where the bathrooms were, and she pointed next door. I walked out and used the bathroom, then I slipped out of the shop and kept on walking down the street until I was at the border. I stood in the line for foot traffic, showed the Border Patrol my passport, and found a bus to Tucson on the other side.

I spent a pleasant evening with my parents. They were relieved to see me in one piece and were polite enough not to ask too many questions. They took me to the Phoenix airport for my flight the next morning. My phone had run out of power, and I didn't have the cord to recharge it. It was in my missing suitcase, but I didn't care about the suitcase or the phone cord. I stretched out across Peter and Stella's two empty seats beside me on the plane and read a book on the way back.

A week after I got back, a friend of Peter's got in touch with me at the hospital. He said that Peter and Stella had been caught on the Mexican border with a small-time drug dealer and were in a Mexican jail.

He said, "I'm going to the Mexican Embassy in London, but it would really help if you could come with me and explain what you were all doing there."

I said, "I don't have much time off right now, and I'm not sure I could explain what we were doing there. Let me think about it and I'll let you know."

FEAR NOT

Laura always had things to worry about, like black widow spiders, water moccasin snakes, rabid dogs, and illegal stills in the horse pasture. Now there was something even worse, a man called the Gaffney Strangler. It was tough being ten years old in South Carolina in 1968. After the strangler had killed two women and a young girl, he called the Gaffney Ledger to say he was going to kill another. Mothers kept their daughters locked in the house, but her mother wasn't afraid. She did remind Laura not to talk to strange men in the deserted parts of the neighborhood. A few days later, when Laura was walking with a friend, she saw a man alone in a beat-up car and they ran away as fast as they could. Her mother always said Laura was the most fearful of the children. Her older sister and brother were reported to be brave. Laura heard that when she was younger, she hid behind her mother's skirts whenever anyone bent down and said, "What a pretty little girl!" She knew girls were supposed to be pretty because she watched her sister compete in beauty contests wearing evening gowns and bathing suits. But Laura didn't want to be the center of attention. Her mother said she was scared of people for no good reason.

~~

She wanted to be a boy because they got preferential treatment. Laura could tell her mother liked her brother better than either of the girls. David was five years older than Laura, and he never had to wash a dish or get up from the table. Even her sister Kate, who was eighteen, brought everything to David while he just sat there. David surrounded himself with a wall of cereal boxes so he wouldn't have to look at Laura during breakfast, but she still thought he was cool. She didn't even tell on him when he stole her favorite Barbie doll. He made her hair black and painted red streaks on her face to turn her into Alice Cooper and hung her from a string to the center of his ceiling. Barbie seemed happy being Alice Cooper. When Laura snuck in to listen to David's Neil Young albums, she pushed the doll to make her swing back and forth across the room. She was afraid to let her mother know when all her Madame Alexander *Little Women* dolls went missing from the top of her dresser and that was a big mistake. When her mother found them in a box, dismembered with their clothes ripped apart and their hair cut off, she blamed it on Laura, but Laura knew David was to blame.

~~

After he killed another girl just like he'd threatened, they caught the Gaffney Strangler. The fifteen-year-old girl was walking to the school bus stop with her sister when the strangler picked her up and threw her into his trunk. Her sister memorized the license plate, and he went away to jail. Laura and Kate both felt safer with him in prison. Soon afterwards, Kate left for college and Laura was lonely. Her father had a new job selling jewelry across the state, so he was often gone too. Because the gold necklaces and diamond rings were so tempting, he carried a gun with him, put alarms on every door and window, and had guns in every room of the house. Laura was worried about robbers. When her family went to restaurants and the jewelry cases were in the trunk of the car, they watched it closely out the windows while they were eating their food.

~~

David started creeping into Laura's room while she was sleeping. When she woke up, she saw him standing near the bed staring at her with an odd look in his eyes. After he started touching her through the covers, she decided to tell her mother. It made her mother mad when she did. She frowned, put down her drink, and told Laura to let her know if it kept happening. The next time it happened, Laura did let her mother know but she was punished. She was sent away to spend a month with her aunt and uncle in Columbia, a bigger town. She didn't like it at first, but her uncle was nice and played Parcheesi with her. At home, no one had ever played games with her before.

~~

Kate got married and went to live in North Carolina. Laura was the one who caught the bouquet after the big wedding. Her friend Gina said it meant Laura would be the next bride, even if she was only eleven. Gina told her that men had parts that poked out like a male dog's pink lipstick, and they stuck them in women to make a baby. She also said that her sister started dripping blood once a month and had to wear something that looked like a diaper and couldn't go swimming.

FEAR NOT

~~

David ran away and was in jail a lot for drugs and drunk driving, but sometimes he came home to drink with her mother. He went crazy with all her father's guns in the house and even shot a hole in the ceiling of his room. Laura continued to stay at her aunt and uncle's house for a month every summer. Her mother told her she was doing them a special favor because her Aunt Mary wasn't able to have children. When Laura turned twelve, she was old enough to take her first communion in the Episcopal church. She had to memorize part of the Prayer Book in order to qualify. She also had to learn how to swallow Christ's body without chewing it first and how to drink from the same cup as everybody else without worrying about the germs. She trained to be an acolyte and liked dressing up in the robes and helping the priest, since mostly only boys got to do it.

~~

The Gaffney Strangler was stabbed and killed in jail by another prisoner. Her father said it served him right. He said child killers never lasted long in jail because the other inmates usually killed them. Laura got her period, and it was a curse just like everybody said it was. Her mother told her she couldn't be an acolyte on the days when she was bleeding because she was unclean. The church seemed more and more like another place for men, where women only cleaned up and arranged the flowers. There were no women included among Christ's disciples, nor in the Father, Son, and Holy Ghost--

unless the Holy Ghost was female. But which woman would the Holy Ghost have been, before she was a ghost?

~~

Her father had a photographer's studio before he went into the jewelry business. One afternoon, he asked Laura to change into a short skirt and took his old equipment out to the porch so he could take pictures of her legs. Then he had her change into a bathing suit for more photos. Her father said, "You're going to be a beautiful broad when you grow up." Laura said, "But Daddy, I want to do something a woman's never done before when I grow up." He said, "Well, I guess you could be the first woman president. Or a woman rapist, since I've never heard of one of those before."

~~

Later that same summer, Laura went to her aunt and uncle's house. Her aunt liked to sleep late, so her uncle took Laura to Shoney's for breakfast the first Saturday. When they finished, he said he needed to drop by his law office. He asked her to give him big hugs while they were there. The same thing happened on the second Saturday, but this time he told her not to mention anything about the office to her aunt. After another uncomfortable session of hugging on the third Saturday, he said he wanted to check and see how her breasts were growing. Laura was scared and stood very still. She was relieved when he only checked her through her clothes. On the fourth Saturday, she pretended to be sick and was happy to go home the next day.

FEAR NOT

~~

Laura ran and hid behind a bush in the neighbor's yard when the first boy called her at home for no good reason. When she came back inside, her father was annoyed with her. He said, "Where'd you go? I told you there was a boy on the phone." Laura asked, "What boy?" "Larry Kaine," her father said, "the son of the dentist in town." "But Daddy, I don't even know him. What's he calling me for?" When her father explained that Larry probably thought she was nice and wanted to get to know her better, Laura said she didn't want to talk to any boys on the phone. Her father said, "Well I'm not going to lie and say you're not here when you are." And Laura said, "Then I guess I'll just run away every time the phone rings." Her mother wasn't going to lie either, so Laura had to run out of the house every time the phone rang. Eventually the game was simplified, so that she only had to hop up and step right outside the door for her parents say she wasn't there. Running away and hiding had interfered too much with her homework.

~~

One night, her parents called Laura to come in and sit down with them while they were having their drinks. Her mother said, "I think it's cruel and heartless not to talk to these boys when they call. They have to summon up all their courage to pick up the phone, and you won't even talk to them." She sipped her gin and tonic and continued, "They're only trying to be nice. I always thought you were considerate and now you're hurting everybody's feelings." Her father asked, "Sugar, what could it possibly be that you're afraid of?" He added, "I bet these boys just want to take you out for something fun like a meal or some ice cream." "And what do they get in return?" Laura asked. Her father said it was 'the pleasure of her company'. She was fairly sure they wanted more than that.

~~

When she turned fifteen, the special *La Pêche* club in town asked Laura to join them because her sister Kate had been a member. On initiation night, the older girls poured rotten food all over them, rubbed grease in their hair, and threw eggs at them hard, which really hurt. When Laura learned the club's main focus was a dance called the Winter Ball, she resigned. She didn't like how it looked when her friends danced with boys and felt too scared and self-conscious to do it herself. She became friends with Amber, a less stuck-up girl in town, and convinced her mother it was safe to drop her off in parking lots for hours at a time to hang out with her friends. They drank Boone's Farm Strawberry Hill wine from the bottle and drove to the more dangerous parts of town. Once, they found a house with girl dolls of all ages, shapes, and sizes hanging by their necks from the trees in the yard. Her friends thought the woman living there had been the wife of the Gaffney Strangler. They all hollered from the truck and threw beer cans in the yard.

~~

When she was due to go to her Aunt Mary's house in July, Laura told her mother she didn't want to go anymore and was met with no resistance. That summer, she read *The Feminine Mystique*, and it confirmed everything she'd already figured out about how women were second-class citizens. Her grades were better than most boys in the class, but she still felt inferior because she wasn't equal. She decided to stop even trying. When tenth grade started, she teamed up with a friend named Louann who had a car. They drank vodka and orange juice on the way to school every morning, and Laura often ended up in the infirmary with headaches before the day was through. She pretended to have a crush on a senior guy who already had a girlfriend and refused to date anyone else. Hanging out with her friends in parking lots was more fun since there were no expectations. Early that spring, a middle-aged man named Peerine started showing up in the lot outside the BI-LO store. He drove a black Camaro and looked like a pinched-face version of Johnny Cash. The boys badgered him, but he didn't seem to mind. When they asked him why he was so weird, he sat silently in his car smiling to himself. One night when his black car glided into place, Laura heard her friend Todd say, "Peerine, you got a gun on your seat. I bet you don't even know how to use it." That was the last thing Todd said. Peerine shot him right in the face.

~~

Laura was sent to an all-girls boarding school in North Carolina the following year. It was the best thing that had ever happened to her. It was a relief to sit in class with only female students and have all women teachers. The girls went to breakfast in their pajamas, played pranks on each other, and had goofy themed parties at night. Laura subscribed to *Ms. Magazine*, joined the National Organization for Women, and started believing in the possibility for change. She found she actually liked dancing when there were only girls around, but still chickened out when it came to boys and dancing at the prom. In her final year there, Laura was the unlucky one who got caught when a group of girls took their newly minted fake ID's to a bar down the street and didn't make it back by curfew. Her trial was a weighty affair for what seemed like such a minor offense. She was first seated alone at one end of a long wooden table and questioned by a panel of her peers. In the evening, she was taken outside where student body officials in white robes carrying candles gathered around to hear her recite a promise to improve. They looked eerily like the Klan; the only thing missing was the hoods. That night, she was taken to the dean's office in the basement where they sat alone and he decided on her punishment. It was the first time she'd met the dean face to face. The hungry look in his eyes made her glad it was the last.

~~

Her father couldn't afford out of state tuition, so Laura had to return to South Carolina for college. He tried to ease her disappointment by giving her a used car. Before she left for college, her mother told Laura that her virginity was her greatest gift, and she should only give it to a man who was incredibly special. Her father gave Laura a sawed-off shotgun to keep in the trunk, in case she had car trouble and someone dangerous came along.

FEAR NOT

~~

The Tri Delta sorority was eager for Laura to join. It was again because of her sister Kate, who had been a devoted member even after college. The friendly sorority house reminded Laura of boarding school, so she agreed. For the initiation, she was blindfolded and guided down the street with the other girls who had been accepted. They were then led into a house and up a difficult flight of stairs and individually escorted to their chairs. Once they were seated, the blindfolds were dramatically removed, and the upper classmen stood before them in togas with cardboard crowns holding tridents. The costumed girls were deadly serious. They took turns reading aloud about the significance of dolphins, the beauty of pansies, and the perfection of pearls, but Laura was too distracted by the outfits to listen. One girl's crown kept falling down over her eyes and another kept dropping her trident.

~~

The Tri Delta's had a tea party on the last Friday of the month, which was held in the sorority house. When Laura dropped by, she was surprised to find that tea was actually served, accompanied by cheese straws and cucumber sandwiches. Laura joked with the sorority president, Claire, and said they should have keg parties like the fraternity houses. The next time tea-party Friday rolled around, a keg was indeed delivered. They played Motown records, sang at the top of their lungs, and danced in lines imitating the moves of the Supremes and the Temptations. Laura even brought over a record by Anita, a soul singer the girls all liked when she was at boarding school.

~~

Claire and Laura became good friends over time, despite the four-year age difference. Claire wasn't your typical sorority girl. She was an accomplished 'pool shark' hustling unsuspecting guys at pool halls around town. Laura couldn't play pool, but she was happy to be Claire's sidekick. First, they both stood close behind the guys at the pool table and complimented them on their shots. Then Claire would say she'd like to play but was embarrassed because she wasn't any good. She would play a couple of games badly for dollar stakes and then bet twenty dollars on the next one. The macho guys at the pool bars would always nod and put their money on the table. It was fun to watch their faces when Claire really started to play. Laura was ready to sprint to the car when Claire grabbed the money and yelled, "Run!"

~~

The next summer, Laura felt lonely when Claire left for law school. Her sister Kate moved from North Carolina to teach English at her college, which was some consolation. Kate was recently divorced and had a two-year-old daughter named Abby. The plan was for Laura to live in the sorority house during the school year and spend the summers with Kate and Abby. Claire did Laura a big favor before she left. Her last task as sorority president was to book Laura's favorite singer, Anita, for the annual Tri Delta dance the following winter. Laura thought she might finally enjoy a dance, especially if Anita performed live. She had managed to go on a few dates with boys during her first year of college, proving to herself it was possible. There was one boy she really liked, but when Laura wouldn't sleep with him, he found another girl who would.

~~

When the time came for the dance, she agreed to go with Steve, a handsome guy she hadn't dated before. She bought a tea-length dark green dress to match her eyes and strapped shoes that were good for dancing. After the white tablecloth dinner, when Anita started to sing on stage, Laura's excitement overcame all her inhibitions, and she didn't care who was watching. She felt free to move and the dancing came naturally. She'd never been as comfortable in her body before. Even when Steve left the dance floor to get drinks, she stayed out there singing and dancing all by herself.

~~

Steve was a good dancer, but he was a bit reserved and shy. After the dance was over, he didn't come along when Laura followed the crowd to a fraternity house down the street. Laura had drunk quite a bit over the evening and was exhausted from all the dancing. At one point, she wandered up the stairs at the fraternity house to go to the bathroom, saw a bed, and decided to lie down for a few minutes. She fell asleep and the next thing she knew there was a guy on top of her. The door to the hallway was closed, and it was too dark to see anything because he had turned out the lights. She kicked out, hit him, and tried to wriggle free, but she wasn't strong enough. He tore off her underwear, pinned her down, and raped her. It was so painful she was immobilized by fear; she didn't dare move in case he decided to do something that hurt her even more. When he pulled up his pants and left the room, she turned away and wept into the pillow. Once she heard him go back down the stairs, she limped to the bathroom and saw that she was bleeding. She made a pad of wadded up toilet paper and had to tie her torn underwear back together to hold it in place. No one noticed her ducking out of the fraternity house door. She hadn't screamed out for help because she'd felt so ashamed and exposed. It was incredibly stupid to have put herself in such a vulnerable place. She should have never let down her guard.

~~

Laura was too humiliated to tell anyone about it afterwards. How could she explain that she'd been raped by a guy she hadn't even seen, and within earshot of everyone downstairs? It was always on her mind--the fraternity was right down the street and she could be passing by the rapist every day. He would know who she was because he saw her when he came in the room before he turned off all the lights. Laura stopped going anywhere but to the grocery store and her classes. She eventually found a winter rental at one of the nearby beaches. It was a small rustic cabin behind a bigger house. She was relieved to escape the sorority house and the campus so she could be alone with her sorrow. It wasn't long before she'd sent a letter of resignation to the sorority. Her friends were sad because they didn't know what happened and wanted to try to help her. But Laura wanted to keep it a secret, so she had to help herself.

FEAR NOT

~~

In the summer, Laura moved into town to live with Kate and Abby in a small house, which wasn't anywhere near the college. She shared a bedroom with Abby, who slept late, even later than she did. Kate was in the master bedroom and had a new boyfriend, Rob, who sometimes spent the night. Kate was teaching summer school at the college, so she left in the mornings and Laura took care of Abby until noon. Abby was a bundle of energy at three years old, so she kept Laura's mind off her troubles in the mornings. But Kate was surprised to find her little sister so depressed in the afternoons when she got home. She asked a few questions, and Laura finally broke down and told her the story. Kate was much more sympathetic than Laura expected. Instead of telling her how stupid she'd been, she hugged her while she cried. The next day, Kate told Laura that Rob knew a good therapist who was also a rape counsellor and asked if Laura would agree to see her. Laura felt betrayed when she heard Kate had told Rob about the rape, but she agreed. Since she didn't want to talk about the rape any more than she had to, she thought one meeting would be all she could handle.

~~

The therapist, Jan, met with Laura at the house. She wore jeans and looked to be in her mid-thirties. Since Laura was reluctant to talk, Jan explained that rapes could lead to all sorts of phobias. She told Laura that if she had irrational fears in the future, it was important to not judge herself too harshly. It was best to unravel and work through them instead. Laura was embarrassed when she started to cry in front of Jan, but the therapist handed her some tissues. Laura said, "I feel like I brought it on myself by doing something stupid." Jan said, "Absolutely not. You were attacked while you were sleeping upstairs. You did nothing to encourage it." The meeting only lasted half an hour but was too wrenching to repeat. Laura wrote a few notes to herself but didn't want to meet with Jan again.

~~

As the summer progressed, Kate and Rob began to spend more time together, and Laura was happy to stay home anytime Abbey needed babysitting. In the past, Rob and Kate had always left the house together in the mornings, but Rob started staying after Kate left for work. This arrangement felt inconvenient for Laura because the bathroom was down the hall from her bedroom, so she had to get dressed every time she used it. Since Rob said he liked having breakfast with Abby, she didn't complain. One day, Laura thought Rob got too close to her in the kitchen. She dismissed it as a phobia because he was so much older. A few mornings later, when Laura came out of her room to go to the bathroom, he was facing her, standing naked, in front of the bathroom door. Instead of apologizing, he smiled. Suddenly, Laura's sadness turned to anger. She screamed, "Get out of here you pervert!" went back in the room with Abby and slammed and locked the door.

FEAR NOT

~~

Once Laura's anger surfaced, it took years to tamp it down. She hated men so much that she enjoyed telling them to fuck-off at the slightest provocation; a man simply sitting down beside her was often enough to set her off. But by the time she finished law school, it had become exhausting to hate half the population. And when she joined a law firm, she found she had male colleagues she really liked. Her fears outlasted all her anger and proved to be the hardest things to overcome. It was ten years before she could be alone in a room with a man and not feel slightly panicked. And she still wanted to be the one who was closest to the door.

~~

Laura eventually fell in love with a wonderful man named Bill, and they had a simple wedding in Gaffney with friends and family. Her parents, her sister and brother, and her aunt and uncle all attended. The wedding ceremony was a joy, but the reception was a trial. Bill always wondered why she made up excuse after excuse not to dance at the reception, and she never told him why. She had never danced again since the night of her rape.

Made in the USA
Middletown, DE
05 May 2021